By ROWAN MCALLISTER

Published by DREAMSPINNER PRESS
http://www.dreamspinnerpress.com

# HOT MESS
## R O W A N
## McALLISTER

*Dreamspinner Press*

Published by
Dreamspinner Press
5032 Capital Circle SW
Suite 2, PMB# 279
Tallahassee, FL 32305-7886
USA
http://www.dreamspinnerpress.com/

Hot Mess
© 2013 Rowan McAllister.

Cover Art
© 2013 L.C. Chase.
http://www.lcchase.com
Cover content is for illustrative purposes only and any person depicted on the cover is a model.

ISBN: 978-1-62798-357-0
Digital ISBN: 978-1-62380-662-0

Printed in the United States of America
First Edition
December 2013

Thanks to M and R for the inspiration.

# CHAPTER ONE

SAM COULDN'T believe his luck. A car pulled out, opening up a spot on the street only two blocks from Java Man. This close to the beach, in summer, that was more than luck—it was a friggin' miracle. Maybe instead of meeting his sister for brunch, he should go buy a lottery ticket.

Before anyone else could take it, Sam pulled his beat-up '95 Cirrus into the open spot, hopped out, and made his way to the sidewalk without bothering to lock the doors. Hermosa Beach wasn't Compton or Lynwood, but anyone who lived within thirty miles of LA knew car locks were pretty pointless. It wasn't a matter of *if* your car got stolen but *when*, so Sam never drove anything he'd be heartbroken to lose.

He'd gotten the Cirrus in trade from a long-time customer who couldn't pay in cash for the parts and labor he needed for his Camaro. The Cirrus had needed a lot of work, and its mottled and patched blue paint job and rusted panels weren't pretty, but it got the job done, and that was really all that mattered. Sam always made sure to park it out of sight at his repair shop so his customers wouldn't be put off when they figured out the owner drove a piece of crap, but beyond that, he didn't care. He'd get his kicks fixing up other people's hot rods and pretty cars and save himself the fear and worry—and insurance premiums—of losing it.

As Sam walked down the sidewalk, listening to his flip-flops slapping the ground and luxuriating in the fact that he was dressed in his favorite ratty cargo shorts and T-shirt instead of his coveralls and

1

work boots—or *worse*, his dress shirt and tie—he felt something coiled tight inside him finally relax. For the first time in longer than he cared to think about, he was actually taking time off from his business and he didn't have to be back there for three whole days. His plan for his vacation was to do absolutely nothing. Well maybe not *nothing*, but as close to it as he could possibly get. And the first stop on his happy relaxation train was great coffee and some much-missed chillin' time with his sister, Elena.

As he came in sight of Java Man, his luck just kept getting better. Elena had managed to snag one of the few tables outside, and there were two large steaming cups already sitting in front of her, along with what he hoped were a couple of his favorite breakfast burritos. He grinned for a second, but then his steps slowed as a little niggle of suspicion started in the back of his mind. It had been a while since they'd gotten together, but he was pretty sure it wasn't her turn to buy. He wasn't going to complain, if she was feeling generous. She could afford it, even with a kid in college. But the last time she'd bought him a meal out of the blue, he'd ended up taking care of her evil cat from hell while she and her family took a three week tour of Europe for his niece's graduation gift.

Sam shrugged off the warning signs. It was a beautiful day. He was back in his home neighborhood, and he had better memories he could be dwelling on than a ball of orange fur with glowing yellow eyes and sharp little needle claws of death. He'd actually been feeling pretty mushy and nostalgic on his drive up, cruising through some of his old high school haunts and the few parks left from when he was a little kid. And now, seeing his sister slouched comfortably in her chair, wearing only a purple-and-red sundress and some brown leather sandals, he was reminded of the bygone days when she used to take him out for ice cream or coffee at least once a week, just to spend time with her little brother. From where he stood, she didn't look much different than she had twenty years ago. Maybe she had to dye her curly sable hair to ward off the gray, and maybe the oversized plastic sunglasses covering her brown eyes also hid a few wrinkles, but in Sam's eyes she'd never change.

Someone bumped into him, and Sam was brought back to the present as he realized he was standing in the middle of the sidewalk staring at his sister with a goofy grin on his face. He apologized to the girl who'd bumped him, even though he didn't know whose fault it was, and stepped into the tiny brick patio and out of the flow of traffic.

Elena's back was to him, so he snuck up on her and gave her a big hug from behind, accompanying it with a smacking, wet kiss on the cheek, simply because he felt like it. She didn't even flinch. She chuckled and raised her eyebrows at him as he straightened and walked around the table.

"Hey, sis," he said as he pulled out the plastic chair across from her and plopped down. He was pretty sure there was still a goofy smile on his face, but he didn't care.

"Hey, baby brother," she replied with a smirk in return.

Sam picked up his mocha and took a sip, without bothering to comment on the "baby brother." He was about to turn thirty, owned his own business, and had been four inches taller than her since junior high, but that didn't seem to matter. Elena was the firstborn, eight years older, and he'd always be the baby, no matter how big he got.

"Glad to finally see you out and about. I was beginning to think you'd crawled under an engine block and died." Elena's opening volley wasn't a surprise. She'd threatened to stage an intervention more than once over the past six months. The little jibe was nothing compared to some of the phone conversations they'd had, so he simply smiled fondly at her and sipped his coffee for a little while before responding.

"Yeah, yeah. I know. All work and no play. I got the message, from you *and* from Ryan *and* from John and yadda yadda. You'll be happy to know, I've not only taken today off, but tomorrow and the next day too." Sam grinned at her exaggerated gasp of surprise. "Yup. And the only thing I have planned is lunch here with you. I don't even have a class at the youth center this week."

"Oh honey, I'm so proud of you," Elena replied with heavy sarcasm, patting his arm condescendingly. "Baby steps. Baby steps." Sam flipped her off, and she laughed for a second before her face sobered. "Seriously. I *am* happy to hear you're coming out of your funk. That asshole, Keith, wasn't worth six months of moping."

Elena hadn't brought up his ex in weeks, and it immediately put Sam on the defensive.

"Hey," he said indignantly, "I wasn't moping, and it wasn't all about Keith, you know. I do have a business to run, and it's doing quite well. Thank you very much."

"Yeah, I know you have the business, and you know how proud I am of you. But you still managed to find time to go out and enjoy yourself, even with the business, when you were dating that putz, so don't give me that bullshit," she shot right back at him.

Sam clamped his lips tight on whatever snippy retort he was going to make. He wouldn't win an argument with her on that subject, especially since she had a point. Besides, he hadn't seen her in forever, and he didn't want to ruin it by bickering over what should have been old news.

"Okay, I yield, sister-mine," he said, raising his hands in surrender. "I will try my hardest to take time to relax and not work myself into an early grave. I promise."

Elena smiled again and slumped back into her chair. "I'm going to hold you to that, especially now school's out and I have more free time to check in on you."

"Speaking of school being out, how's that empty-nest syndrome going?" Sam asked with a laugh, hoping to lighten the mood as he unwrapped his burrito.

Elena's only child, Shawna, had gone off to college the previous fall, and it had taken his sister and her husband, Michael, months to adjust to the peace and quiet… right about the time Shawna came home for winter break. At which point, the fighting had begun over house rules and Shawna's newly found desire for independence. That first week, Sam had received several tear-filled phone calls from his niece and his sister both. He'd still been reeling from his breakup with Keith, and trying to deal with that and be supportive, while not getting himself into a heap of trouble with either female, had been interesting.

He hadn't heard much from either one since Shawna had come home for summer break, so he was hoping things had calmed down enough for Elena to laugh about it now. But instead of the pained smile or rude hand gestures he was expecting in response to his question, his sister slumped down a little further in her chair and bit her lip. She looked so grave and guilty Sam knew something big was up. He set his burrito back down on the table, without taking a bite.

Elena set her coffee cup down too and pushed her sunglasses up. "Well, actually, that was one of the reasons I asked you out today. I was going to wait until after we ate to bring it up, but you beat me to it."

He couldn't ignore the warning bells anymore. "Okay, what's up?"

She grabbed her paper cup again and tapped it on the table a few times before raising her gaze to Sam's. "I hate to do this to you, now that you've finally decided to start taking some time for yourself again, but I need to ask you a favor. It's a big one, so I want you to think about it before you answer."

"You know I'd do anything for you, El."

She shook her head. "I know you would. That's why I really want to make sure you know it's okay to say no this time. I feel guilty enough asking. I don't want you to feel like you have to say yes just because it's me."

"Will you quit beating around the bush and tell me what it is so I can agree already? Sheesh, you're making me nervous, hedging like this. It's not like you."

Elena chuckled. "Yeah, I know. We're usually pretty blunt, aren't we? Okay. Here goes. The reason I haven't had empty-nest syndrome again, even before Shawna came home, is because my nest is a little too full at present. Not only do I have Shawna, but I have someone else staying with us, and it's not quite working out." She grimaced and took another sip of her coffee before continuing. "His name is Cameron. He was a student of mine, until he dropped out halfway through the year. He had some trouble at home, and he moved in with some guy in West Hollywood. But the guy was bad news and Cameron came to live with me a month or so ago so he could try to get his shit back together."

"El." Sam sighed and shook his head. His sister had one of the biggest hearts of anyone he'd ever known. She came off tough as nails, but she let people walk all over her sometimes. Sam would give her shit about it, but, in all honesty, it would be a case of pot calling kettle, since he was as much of a pushover for a sob story as she was.

"He's a really good kid, Sam. He's smart and creative. I could tell he had real talent as a writer when he was in my class, and I hated it when he up and disappeared. He just turned twenty, and he still has real problems at home, but where he was staying was even worse, so when he called me out of the blue to ask for help, I didn't have the heart to say no." Elena shrugged and grimaced again. "Michael was already pretty pissed I told Cameron he could stay with us without consulting him first. And now that Shawna's home, he's pushing for me to kick Cameron out, like *yesterday*. But the kid doesn't have anywhere to go, and I'm afraid of what kind of trouble he'll get into if he's out on his own again."

"You're asking me to take him?" It wasn't really a question. Sam already knew the answer. If Michael wanted the kid gone, he'd be hell to live with until it happened, and Elena would be caught between trying to do what she thought was right and trying to keep her family happy. Sam could almost picture Michael's face when he'd come home to find his wife had brought home a stray. Uptight WASP that he was, he'd probably almost burst a blood vessel. Sam kind of wished he'd been a fly on the wall for that one, except for how hard it must have been on his sister.

"I'm asking you to think about it, yes," she said after a few moments. "He *is* a really great kid. I just want him to have a chance at the future he deserves."

Sam frowned. "Twenty is hardly a kid, El. Doesn't he have *anyone* he can go to? There are shelters out there…." He didn't want to be a jerk, but taking a stranger into his home was a pretty big step. The kid—scratch that—*young man* must have made some kind of impression for her to go that far to help him out.

She shook her head. "He doesn't have anyone. From what he's told me, and what I learned from his records at school, Cameron's mom's a drunk. He and his stepdad don't get along at all, especially since Cameron came out to them, and Cameron's dad is in jail for some kind of securities fraud or some other white-collar thing. He doesn't have anywhere else, Sam. The guy he was staying with was a real user, in his fifties, a partier with a taste for young guys. Cameron needs someplace stable. I know shelters are an option, but I don't think he'll do very well at one of them. I'd rather not go there unless there's no other choice. And frankly, I doubt he'd stay at a shelter for very long. He'd probably end up falling back in with the crowd he's trying to get away from."

*And cue the violins.*

Sam sighed, closed his eyes, and brought a hand up to rub his forehead. So Cameron was from a broken home, and probably kicked out because he was gay, and then fell into the clutches of a predator. Great. Add to that the fact Elena really seemed to care about the guy, and there was no way Sam could say no.

Yep, bleeding hearts ran in his family like nobody's business.

"Sam—" she started, but he held up his hand to stop her.

"No more. You got me. So how long are we talking about here?"

She let out the breath she'd apparently been holding and smiled fondly at him. "You're the best, baby brother. And once more for the record, Keith was a complete idiot for ever letting you go."

Actually Keith had walked out, and Sam had been the one who had to do the "letting go," but he wasn't going to quibble over semantics, not when his sister was paying him a compliment. He'd heard the same sentiments from her and the rest of his friends dozens of times over the last six months, but his ego still appreciated the stroking.

Sam smiled and repeated his question. "How long?"

"Just until he gets on his feet. He needs his GED, if he's going to go on to college or get any kind of decent job, so that's first. But I'm sure he can get something to help with the bills in the meantime. We picked up some prep books already, and he should only have to study a little to brush up on what he missed. Maybe, if you give him the summer to figure things out?"

A couple of months wouldn't kill him. He hoped.

"Okay. I've got the time off now, so you might as well bring him by tonight. But if he robs me blind or burns my house down, I'm blaming you. Just remember that."

She bounced up out of her seat and rushed around the table to wrap her arms around his shoulders and plant a big kiss on his cheek. "Thanks, Sam. You won't be sorry." She sat back down and stretched her legs out under the table, smiling broadly. "Now that's out of the way, we can relax and catch up on all the wonderful and fantastic things going on in our lives. You first."

Needless to say, Sam didn't have a whole lot to contribute to that part of the conversation. His business was doing well enough for him to be able to promote his supervisor, Cesar, to assistant manager, so he could finally hand over some of the responsibility of running the place. He'd gotten some pretty cool "thank you" letters in the last month from a few of the kids in his classes at the youth center who'd gone on to get accepted to auto tech programs. But other than that, things were pretty quiet. He could tell by the look on his sister's face it hadn't escaped her notice he'd skipped over sharing anything of a romantic nature, and he knew the next question was coming before she even opened her mouth.

"Do you need me to call Ryan and get him to set you up on some dates, or are you going to get back on the horse yourself?"

"I can find my own dates, *mamá*." He shot back, using the one word in his arsenal guaranteed to piss her off. Keith may have dented his self-confidence a little by dumping him for some hot, young party-boy, but Sam wasn't a total loser in the romance category. He might not be an Adonis, but he was still in pretty good shape, and he wasn't all that bad to look at either.

"Well go out and find some, then," she huffed.

"Can we talk about something other than my love life, please?"

She rolled her eyes. "Fine."

At least she knew when to stop pushing, though he knew she was dying to. They talked for a little while longer and ate their burritos and drank their coffees. Elena caught him up on all the news about Shawna and Michael, their vacation plans for the summer, and family gossip before hugging him good-bye and driving off to go tell her houseguest the news.

After she left, Sam decided not to go down to the beach like he'd originally planned. Instead, he headed home to Long Beach so he could clear out the only guest bedroom he had in preparation for his new roommate. Elena called a couple of hours later to tell him they'd be showing up after dinner that night. Sam had just enough time to truly regret agreeing to do this when his doorbell rang, announcing their arrival.

He groaned as he bent down to pick up the last box of papers and memorabilia he'd stored in his tiny spare room. Everything he'd moved out was pretty much junk he probably should have gotten rid of a long time ago. But he didn't feel like dealing with it now, so he'd moved it to the carport to make room for his guest. At least the stuff was one step closer to the curb, even if he wasn't prepared to make that final commitment.

He set the last box on the coffee table in the living room and went to open the door with a big welcoming smile on his face—a smile that froze in place when he got his first look at his houseguest to be.

*Holy shit, El, I'm going to kill you.*

The kid standing next to his sister didn't look more than sixteen years old, complete with low-rise skinny jeans, neon-orange oversized belt, skintight striped polo that rode up to show off his belly-button stud, a matching set of snakebites in his lips, and messy, razor-cut hair, dyed black and combed into his face—a face that looked way too pretty for his own good. The guy probably barely weighed a hundred pounds soaking wet, and Sam could almost hear social services banging on his door already.

"Sam?" Elena's voice brought him out of his shocked stupor long enough to realize he was staring rudely at her charge.

"Uh, sorry. Come on in."

Elena and Cameron walked past him into the living room and waited while he shut the door. Cameron carried only a backpack and a small duffel bag, which he set on the floor at his feet. Chewing on one of his lip rings, he looked nervously around Sam's house.

"Sam. I'd like you to meet Cameron Lacey. Cameron, this is my brother, Samuel Emilio Powell," Elena introduced them.

Out of habit, Sam extended his hand, and after only a moment's pause, Cameron shook it. The kid's hand felt small and thin in his palm, making Sam feel huge in comparison, which was no mean feat, considering Sam was only five-ten, with a pretty average build.

"Nice to meet you, Cameron," he managed to say, despite his growing anxiety over what his sister had gotten him into. He didn't want to think Elena had lied to him, but it was really hard for him to buy that this kid was over eighteen years old.

"You too," Cameron said in a light tenor before letting his hand drop back to his side and chewing on his lip ring again without another word.

Elena gave Sam a look that said, *"say something!"* so Sam quashed his concerns for the moment and cleared his throat.

"Why don't you come with me, and I'll show you your room?"

Sam led the way down the hall, and Cameron followed him into the spare bedroom.

"I cleared out the closet and the dresser, and there's clean sheets on the futon. The bathroom is right across the hall."

When all he got was a mumbled "thanks" from Cameron, Sam clenched his teeth. "I'll leave you to get settled. Come on out when you're ready, and I'll give you the rest of the tour."

Sam tried not to stomp as he made his way back to his sister. She was in the kitchen, getting herself a glass of lemonade, when he found her. "Jesus, El, are you trying to get me arrested?" he hissed at her, making an effort to keep his voice down so Cameron didn't overhear.

She frowned at him. "What are you talking about?"

Sam rolled his eyes. "There's no way that kid is legal, El."

Elena rolled her eyes right back at him. "You're too young to be that far out of touch, Sam. It's those of us who're pushing forty or fifty that are supposed to go on and on about how kids are looking younger and younger these days." She chuckled at her own joke and took a sip of her lemonade, but when he continued to glare at her, she sighed. "I've seen his records, Sam. He was eighteen at the beginning of his senior year with me. He was even a grade behind because he flunked his freshman year—I'm guessing because of whatever happened with his dad going to jail, since he's certainly smart enough he shouldn't have had any trouble with the work. I'm telling you, he's twenty. I promise."

Sam grabbed the glass out of his sister's hand and finished it off as he tried to make himself relax. The kid was legal. He wasn't going to get hauled off for child endangerment or something. No angry parents were going to come after him and take every penny he had for corrupting their son. He could do this.

The upside in all of this was Sam definitely didn't go for the "barely legal" type, and he was almost positive a kid that pretty wouldn't go for an almost-thirty, average Joe like himself, so there wasn't going to be any sexual tension to complicate things.

"Okay. Okay. I believe you. Let's go finish getting him settled in," he said as he handed the empty glass to his sister and walked back into the living room.

# CHAPTER TWO

CAMERON DROPPED his duffel on the floor and his backpack on the futon behind him before slumping onto the mattress himself and letting out a breath he hadn't realized he was holding. The house wasn't quite what he was used to, but it was neat, and well cared for, and so very *average* he found himself liking it, despite its lack of luxury.

The look he'd first gotten from Sam, like the guy was wondering what rock Cameron had crawled out from under, had made him want to cut and run. But Sam had seemed to loosen up a bit as he led Cam back to what was going to be his room, and Cameron was able to let go of some of his nerves.

*Sam's gay,* he reminded himself as he looked around the mostly empty room. He knew how to handle gay men, and a lot of supposedly straight men too. Even if Cameron wasn't exactly Sam's type, that didn't mean the guy wouldn't take a blowjob or a hand job here or there, if it was offered. Elena had gone on and on about how nice her brother was, but Cameron knew the score. Sam had a dick, and even "good guys" liked to get laid as often as possible. Cameron was living proof of that. Sam wasn't exactly a hottie, but he wasn't a troll either. He had a nice face, square jaw, cleft chin, and a decent set of brown eyes that matched his hair. A small tattoo of a sun peaked out from his ratty T-shirt, saving him from being too vanilla, and his nose had a bump at the top, like it'd been broken and hadn't been set properly, which Cam kind of liked. It was a nice change from all the perfect faces and bodies he was used to in the Hollywood club scene. He'd have to take a little time to feel Sam out, find out what the guy was into, and then he was sure they'd get along great, at least until Cameron could finish his GED and finally get his ass back on track and living on his own terms… whatever the hell those were.

He took a deep breath and stood up, stuffing his fingers into the tiny pockets of his too-tight jeans so neither Sam nor Elena could see his hands shake as he made his way back to the living room.

*You can do this. There's no reason to freak.*

He continued the little mantra in his head as he did the breathing exercises one of his therapists had taught him years ago to help with his bouts of anxiety.

Sam and Elena were in the living room when he came back out. They both looked up at him and smiled as he walked into the room. Elena's smile was a bit warmer than Sam's, but Cameron could fix that in time. If he knew anything, it was how to make a man smile.

"All settled in?" Elena asked.

"Yeah. It's great. Thanks for letting me stay, Sam."

Sam's brown eyes softened a little, and his smile got warmer. "It's no problem. Why don't we all go sit on the deck, drink some lemonade, and just hang out for a bit before El has to head home?"

*Lemonade on the back deck? Was he serious?*

Cameron felt like he was in a rerun of *Leave It to Beaver* or something.

Elena led the way out a set of sliding glass doors at the far end of the living room, to a small, worn wooden deck, in a tiny, fenced-in backyard, complete with tidy little flower beds along the fence line and a perfectly clipped square of grass. Obviously Sam wasn't rolling in dough, but the little bungalow on its postage stamp of a yard was cute. Cameron could almost hear the sitcom theme music in his head as Sam came out with a tray of lemonade. And a moment later, Cameron swore he could hear the laugh track when Sam lost his balance, after using his foot to push the door closed, and hopped his way to the little rusty metal table as he tried to right himself, sloshing the lemonade onto the tray. The whole scene was so TV Land it was freaking Cameron out, but in a good way.

"Almost lost it," Sam laughed as he handed out the glasses.

Elena rolled her eyes. "You could've asked for help, you know."

"That would have robbed you of my stunning entrance," Sam shot back, even as his cheeks flamed red beneath his tan.

Elena shook her head, and Cameron smiled at the back and forth, hiding his grin behind his lemonade so Sam wouldn't think he was laughing at him. Guys typically didn't like being laughed at.

Sam sat down and took a sip from his glass before clearing his throat and looking at Cameron. "Now that we're all settled, I guess we should talk a little about your plans, Cameron, so we're all on the same page."

He'd known it was coming, but he still tensed up once the question was out there. Elena's husband, Michael, had insisted on sitting him down for "the talk," not long after he'd gotten to their house. The guy had been such a douche about it, Cameron had stammered out some completely stupid bullshit, and the asshole had only used it as more proof Cameron shouldn't be allowed to stay with them anymore. Cam had no idea what a great lady like Elena saw in a tight-ass like Michael, but the love lives of the straight and narrow weren't really his line of expertise. At least Sam was trying to be nice about it, which made Cameron want to be honest.

"I don't know." He dropped his gaze to his glass and scraped at a chip of paint on the tabletop with one of his nails. "I've got the GED prep books, and I'm doing pretty well at catching up. I should be able to take the test soon, and then I might have a better chance at getting a job while I look into what I need for community college." That plan *sounded* decent at least, even if he wasn't completely sure he could do it.

Elena gave him an approving smile and patted his knee under the table.

"Okay, that sounds like a good start," Sam said. "I'm guessing you don't have a car?"

Cameron shook his head. His mom and stepdad had kept it when they'd kicked him out.

Sam pursed his lips. "I guess I can help you out a little bit with rides, but I work a lot of long hours, so you're going to have to get to know the bus system. There's a pretty good one around here, despite the fact no one ever deigns to use it. You might have to limit your job search to areas you can get to that way, at least for the time being."

Cam nodded, because he assumed that's what Sam wanted. He wasn't completely helpless or an idiot, but he knew the guy was only trying to be helpful, so he didn't roll his eyes, like he wanted to. The bus was going to take some getting used to, but he was pretty sure he could figure that part out on his own.

The silence stretched awkwardly after that as all three of them drank their lemonade and Cameron tried to come up with something to say. In the end, under his sister's expectant stare, Sam was the one to break it. "El says you're a pretty good writer. Is that what you're thinking of taking classes for?"

Cameron shook his head and brushed his bangs out of his face. "No. I was thinking maybe psychology. I can't think of anything else I have as much experience with." Cam laughed at his own private joke, and Sam gave him a blank look.

After another awkward minute, the guy cleared his throat and motioned to the big neon-orange-and-black headphones Cameron had dangling around his neck. "What kind of music do you like?"

He shrugged. "Pretty much everything, as long as it has good vocals or a good beat—club music, pop, alternative, some classic rock, and even a little country, if I'm in the right mood."

Sam smiled and relaxed against the back of his chair. "You'll have to show me what you've got sometime. If you like classics, we might have some favorites in common."

Cameron beamed at him and nodded, feeling like he'd just scored some points. He'd seen the acoustic guitar on the stand in the corner of Sam's living room, when he'd first walked in the front door. "Do you play?" he asked, pointing at it through the sliding glass doors.

Sam glanced over his shoulder. "A little. Our dad was the real musician in the family. That was his. I can strum enough simple chords to get through some of my favorites, but that's about it."

15

Elena looked behind her and smiled fondly at it too. "*Mamá* used to say it was the only reason she ever fell for a *gringo*. He was on that thing at every party we ever had, growing up. I used to be so embarrassed, until all my girlfriends started mooning over him. Then I was *completely mortified*."

They all laughed and the brief silence that followed didn't seem quite so awkward anymore. Elena had never mentioned her father before, but it was pretty obvious the man must be dead from the way they talked about him, gone but very much missed. Cameron supposed there had to be a few dads in the world worth missing, even if he'd never actually met one himself.

They talked a little more about music before Elena finished off her lemonade in one long gulp and set her glass down. "It seems like you guys might get along without me now, so I'm going to go home and make sure Shawna and her dad haven't killed each other over the TiVo." She stood up and both men followed her into the house. "See you later, baby brother," she said as she gave Sam a hug and a kiss by the front door. "Cameron, why don't you walk me out?"

Cameron chewed on his lip and stuffed his hands back in his pockets as he followed her out the door and across the little front yard to her car. Elena was a sweet lady most of the time, and as a general rule, older ladies liked him for some weird reason, but he wasn't very good at predicting what she wanted from him or which way her mood would turn. His experience with women was pretty limited, and he couldn't exactly draw on his mom as an example of how a normal woman acted… or maybe he could, but that was too depressing to think about.

She turned around when they reached the side of her car and regarded him seriously for a moment. "Cameron, you know I still want to help you, right?" At his nod, she reached out and gave him a quick hug. "Good. I know things got a little tense at the house with Michael, but I also really think you'll be better off here with Sam. He's a great guy. He built his own business up from the wreck of a back alley shop our uncle Julio left him, so he knows how to make his way in the world. You could learn a lot from him." She paused and waved her hands dismissively. "I know I told you all of this before, but I want you to know you can trust him. And I know he has a lot of friends at the youth center where he volunteers. If psychology is the way you want to go, one of them might even be able to help you find a job, until you're done with school. Talk to him. He wants to help."

Cameron nodded, feeling a little overwhelmed all of a sudden. "I will," he said, because he knew it was what she wanted to hear.

He gave her another quick hug before stepping back so she could get in her car. He waved as she drove away, and took a deep breath before turning to go back to the house. Sam was waiting in the living room. He was sitting on the back of his couch with his arms crossed and a serious expression on his face.

"So, uh, I guess we should go over a few ground rules about the house," Sam said. His voice was gentle, but Cameron couldn't help tensing up a bit.

"Okay."

"I don't want to be a hard-ass or anything, but there are a few important things to know, if you're going to stay here. First is, I'm okay with you having a friend or two over, but you need to ask me beforehand, especially if they're going to be here when I'm not. There won't be any parties, and you're responsible for anything your friends do in my house."

Cameron nodded. He'd been avoiding his so-called friends anyway. He was trying to turn over a new leaf, and there was no way he'd be able to do it if he partied with the guys he used to hang out with.

"Second, I'm not your maid," Sam continued. "I'm not a neat freak, but my place is too small to let it get messy. There's only the one bathroom, and as you can see, the kitchen's pretty tiny." He waved a hand in the direction of the small breakfast bar that divided the living room from the kitchen. The man wasn't exaggerating. It was tiny. "We'll figure out how to share chores as we go along. But I'm not picking up after you. You do your own dishes and your own laundry. Got it?"

"Got it."

Sam's smile was back. "Good. Do you know how to cook?"

Cameron squirmed. "Do frozen pizzas and microwave burritos count?"

Sam rolled his eyes. "Guess I'm going to have to teach you. I'm too old to live off that shit without getting fat, and if I'm working late or teaching my class, and you're going to be here all day, that job is going to fall on you."

The look on Cameron's face must have been priceless, because Sam threw back his head and laughed. "Don't worry. I'll make it simple stuff. Give you some easy recipes to follow. If you're as smart as El thinks you are, you'll figure it out."

Cameron watched in surprise as Sam headed back out to the deck, cleared the tray of lemonade and empty glasses from the table, and carried them into the kitchen. Despite his initial impression, Cameron had to admit, Sam was almost sexy when he laughed. He let his eyes follow the muscles of Sam's throat, down to the opening of his shirt in appreciation for a second or two. He usually went for skinny, young guys, like himself, but he was starting to get curious about what a guy like Sam would have to offer. It had been weeks since he'd gotten laid, and it never took much for Cameron to get horny. As he watched the man put glasses into the dishwasher and return the pitcher to the refrigerator, he found himself wondering what Sam would look like without the bulky green cargo shorts and the ratty yellow T-shirt he was wearing.

Cameron propped his elbows on the island and let his eyelids droop a little in appreciation as he peered up at Sam from beneath his bangs. "Isn't there anything I could do to get out of it?"

Sam laughed as he turned around, but then his eyes widened and frown lines creased his forehead. The smile slowly fell from his face, but he looked more puzzled than angry, like he was trying to figure out exactly what Cam was trying to say. Not Cameron's most successful attempt at flirting, but at least he'd gotten the guy's attention.

Sam paused a few beats before shaking his head, rolling his eyes, and chuckling. "Nope. Dinner is going to be on you at least half the time. Come on. Let me show the wonders of the laundry room, and then I might let you kick my ass on the Xbox for an hour or so before I go to bed." He led the way through a door off the back of the kitchen as Cameron chewed on his lip and tried to swallow his disappointment.

It wasn't as if he really had the hots for the guy, but he didn't like getting the brush-off either. And he was still horny.

Cameron gave a purely internal sigh and tried to get his mind off sex, as Sam explained the glories of his washer and dryer. Maybe he'd have to be a little less subtle next time. Or maybe he should simply get Sam drunk and see if that would make him drop the big brother act so they could get back on some familiar ground. Sam was being too nice for Cameron's comfort. Nobody in this world gave you something for nothing. It just didn't happen.

# CHAPTER THREE

AFTER SAM finished with the nickel tour of his little house, he led Cameron back out into the living room, and they sat down on the couch and played *Call of Duty* for a couple of hours. Despite his earlier freak-out, Sam was starting to feel optimistic. It was kind of nice having someone in the house again. The tiny bungalow had been all too empty after Keith left, and Sam hadn't had time to invest in starting a new relationship since then. Maybe having Cameron stay with him would be good for both of them.

He'd had serious doubts that afternoon. Things had been a bit awkward, and there was a moment in the kitchen when Sam thought the kid was actually flirting with him. But after a few hours of gaming, Sam was sure Cameron had only been kidding around, and the rest of the evening was good, better than good. Cameron was a sweet kid. He was bright, polite, and a little goofy when he finally relaxed—geeking out and talking smack like only another gaming dork could. And despite the fact Cameron did indeed kick his ass on the game, several times over, Sam had more fun that night than he'd had in weeks.

THE NEXT morning, Sam wasn't surprised he was the first one up. Despite the fact he had the day off, his body was still on shop-time, and Cameron was at that stage in his life where he probably hadn't seen a morning in months. The coffee pot was set on a timer, so all Sam had to do was fill his cup before heading out to the deck to enjoy another leisurely morning. Unfortunately, as the sun rose above the lemon trees in his neighbor's yard, Sam could already feel himself getting antsy. He wasn't used to having nothing to do.

One of the good things about not having a boyfriend or a social life was he had plenty of time to do maintenance on the house, even when he was working a minimum of six days a week. But that left him at loose ends when he did something as crazy as taking three whole days off in a row. It was just as well Elena had asked him to take Cameron in, otherwise he might have been tempted to go in to work when he got too stir-crazy at home. Now, he couldn't really leave Cameron alone in his house on his first full day there, so he *had* to stay home.

Sam drank the rest of his coffee and tried to force himself to relax and appreciate the benefits of all the hard work he'd put in over the past few years. He had a great house, all his now that Keith had moved on to greener pastures. He had a thriving business and great friends and family. He had money set aside if he needed it. Other than a boyfriend, what more could a man ask for?

Listing all the things he had to be thankful for took up approximately ten minutes of Sam's morning, and then he was left with that antsy feeling again. Sitting still wasn't his thing. He'd been crazy to schedule three days off without even a class to teach or some sort of plans with his friends. What the hell was he thinking?

As Sam was wracking his brain, trying to think of something to do with his day, he heard footsteps in the living room, announcing his guest was finally up and moving. With a sigh of relief, Sam got up and carried his mug back inside for a refill as a sleepy, but surprisingly well groomed, Cameron shuffled into the kitchen.

Cameron certainly didn't look like he'd just rolled out of bed. Sam was expecting some pajamas or a T-shirt and shorts, at least some bed head, but Cameron was fully dressed in an outfit similar to the one he'd worn the day before—except the belt was neon green this time, matching the gauges in his ears, and the skinny jeans were white and artfully shredded. Sam glanced down at his own faded boxers and ragged T-shirt, feeling underdressed all of a sudden.

"Morning," Cameron said, covering a yawn with his hand.

"Good morning. I'm guessing you slept well, since you're already up and ready for the day."

Cameron shrugged. "Yeah. It took me a little while to get to sleep because your neighborhood's a little busier than I'm used to, but I slept pretty good. Can I have some coffee?"

Sam stepped out of the way. "Help yourself. There's milk in the fridge and sugar in the bowl by the stove. If you like creamer or anything like that, you can write it down. I'll probably go to the store today or tomorrow while I'm off."

Cameron walked past him, brushing against his side as he came around the breakfast bar. The scent of perfumed bodywash or cologne reached his nostrils, and Sam arched an eyebrow. The kid was barely awake. Why had he bothered getting dressed and primped so early? Maybe he was still nervous about being too casual around Sam, or maybe he was vain enough to never let anyone see him in anything but his best?

Sam would never understand the younger generation's obsession with fashion. There was less than ten years difference between them, but it felt like twenty when he looked at the effort Cameron had put into his appearance, even before he'd had a cup of coffee. As if to punctuate that point, the rhinestone ball on the end of Cameron's belly button stud winked at Sam as Cameron reached up into the cabinet for a mug and his tight shirt rode up.

Sam shook his head. Maybe it didn't have anything to do with age. Maybe he was simply clueless about fashion. All that shit had never meant much to him. Of course, that might be why he was turning thirty and still single, so it was possible the kid knew something he didn't.

"Do you have any big plans for the day?" Sam asked as he looked away from Cameron's bare midriff.

Cameron shrugged as he set the mug down and poured his coffee. "I thought I might check out the bus schedule and maybe scope out the nearest library. I forgot to ask you for the Wi-Fi password last night so I could get online with my laptop, but sometimes it's just easier to find what I need in the library anyway. They usually have all the GED prep books—including the ones I don't already have—together in one place, and it's easier to skim them in hardcopy."

"I wasn't sure if you had a computer or not. Sorry, I should have thought to ask before we went to bed."

Cameron shrugged again as he finished doctoring his coffee with way too much milk and sugar, brushed by Sam a little too closely again, and climbed onto one of the stools at the breakfast bar. "It's no biggie. I had my phone, if I needed to check anything that desperately. My mom still pays for it, so I'm not completely without. She may have let '*the asshole*' kick me out, but she can't cut me off completely."

Sam set his mug on the counter and leaned back against it, facing Cameron across the bar. "El said something about that yesterday, but I didn't get much detail. Are things that bad between you and your folks?"

"Between me and my mom and *stepdad*," Cameron corrected. "And yeah, it got ugly. My mom's always been a lush, and being married to '*the asshole*' hasn't helped. Dear old Arthur and I never got along, and after I came out, it only got worse." Cameron paused there and chewed one of his lip rings for a minute before sighing and raising his thickly lashed hazel eyes to Sam's. Was he wearing mascara? Sam couldn't tell. "It isn't all their fault, I guess. I was partying pretty hard and messing up in school, the last few months I was there. We fought a lot, but neither one of them really made an effort to help. Mom drank more and avoided me, and Art flipped out and yelled until he finally just threw me out." He dropped his gaze then and wrapped his thin fingers around his coffee. The large glass ring on his middle finger clinked against the mug.

"Do you think it might be worth talking to them again, now you've gotten away from all that and are working on getting back on track?"

Cameron shook his head, and then brushed his bangs out of his eyes as his mouth twisted bitterly. "I called the day I walked out of Sean's place in West Hollywood for good. I only got a few words in with my mom before '*the asshole*' took her phone and hung up on me. That's when I called Mrs. Spencer—Elena." He shrugged and glanced up at Sam again. "You're not trying to get rid of me already are you?" Cameron laughed as he said it, but Sam could see the concern in his eyes.

"No. Like I said, El didn't really go into much detail, so I thought I should ask. That's all. I'm not kicking you out." Cameron still looked a little tense, so Sam decided to lay off the personal questions for a while. "Are you hungry?"

Cameron shrugged again. Sam was beginning to think he'd see a lot of that particular gesture in the days to come. It seemed to be one of Cameron's favorites. "A little."

Sam smiled. "Then come on over here, and I'll give you your first cooking lesson. How do you like your eggs?"

Cameron studied him for a few seconds, like he was trying to figure out if Sam was serious or not. But when Sam raised his eyebrows and held out the spatula he'd grabbed from the jar on the counter, Cameron rolled his eyes playfully and slowly slid off the stool. He stepped in a little too close again, looking up at Sam expectantly through his bangs, and Sam took a step back and shoved the spatula at him. "Hold on to that."

When Cameron took it from him, Sam squeezed around his guest to get the eggs and butter out of the fridge. Cameron continued to hover closer than Sam was used to, as he bent down to pull out a pan from the drawer beneath the oven, but Sam figured the kid must have a different definition of personal space than most people. Growing up, Sam's family had been all over one another, plenty of hugs and kisses and cuddling, but Keith had liked to have his space, even when they'd first gotten together, so it had been a long time since Sam lived with someone who had even fewer boundaries than he did.

"So you didn't answer. How do you like your eggs?" Sam asked.

"Scrambled is fine."

Sam pulled out a bowl and a whisk and set them on the counter. Handing over the carton of eggs, he said, "Get cracking."

Cameron rolled his eyes at Sam's bad joke and awkwardly began breaking open the eggs over the bowl, swearing and fishing out pieces of shell each time he did it.

Sam held back the laughter that threatened to break loose, but he couldn't help smiling. "You seriously haven't ever made your own eggs?"

Cameron shrugged again. "The guy I was living with, Sean, had a cook. And when I was a kid, I could make myself a bowl of cereal. Every once in a while, my mom would get on a domestic kick, set the booze aside for an hour or so, and cook a big breakfast, but it never turned out well, and it was best to stay out of the way. Mostly, I just scrounged around when I was hungry and developed a fondness for microwave burritos. My dad had a housekeeper who cooked for us."

Sam handed over the whisk and the milk as the phrase "poor little rich kid" ran uncharitably through his head. He pushed it away, though, because the kid may have had it easy growing up like that, but it left him completely unable to take care of himself now his life had gone to shit. "Pour a couple of dollops of milk in there and stir it up, until the yolks are all broken and mixed in." Cameron did as he was told, and Sam said, "I'm sorry about your dad. Elena told me he was sent away when you were only a freshman. That had to be hard."

Cameron stopped stirring the eggs and tensed up. "Yeah, well. It was a long time ago. So are you going to show me how to cook these things or what?"

*Okay, so Cameron's a little sensitive about his dad. Good to know.*

"The pan's hot. Put in a little butter to keep the eggs from sticking and pour them in. Use the spatula to scrape the cooked bits off the bottom, until they clump up and cook through and that's it. You've cooked your first breakfast."

Sam stepped back and leaned against the breakfast bar while Cameron stirred his eggs. He was still curious about Cameron's family, but it wasn't really his business to pry. They might talk about it later, when they'd gotten to know each other a little better.

Sam watched Cameron for a minute or so before he put a couple of pieces of bread in the toaster and went back to his place by the breakfast bar, giving the kid some space and a little time to let go of some of the tension their conversation had obviously caused.

The smile of triumph Cameron gave him as he scooped his eggs onto the plate Sam got out for him was well worth leaving his curiosity unsatisfied, and Sam found himself smiling broadly back. "See, simple. All you have to do is cut up some veggies or mushrooms into it and wait until the eggs are mostly cooked through before using the spatula to flip the whole thing over, throw on some cheese, and you've cooked us an omelet for dinner. Or, even easier still, grease a big cast iron pan, pour the eggs and stuff in, put some cheese on top, and throw it into the oven for a half hour or so, until it doesn't jiggle when you shake the pan, and you've got a frittata."

Cameron stopped eating and gave Sam a look like he didn't believe it was as easy as Sam was making it sound, and Sam laughed. "Trust me. I'll make a cook out of you yet."

The kid peered up at him through his eyelashes and smiled. "If anyone can do it, I'm sure it's you," he said and actually winked. Sam raised an eyebrow but shrugged it off. Cameron was just being a smartass.

Sam cooked a couple of eggs for himself and finished them off with the second piece of toast. When Cameron came around the counter with his plate, he still seemed a little tense and vulnerable from their previous conversation, so, on impulse, Sam put his plate down and wrapped his arms around his houseguest's shoulders, giving him a quick squeeze. "It's going to be okay, Cameron. El and I are here to help. You're not on your own."

Cameron gave him a weird look, and Sam wondered if he'd crossed a line. Given the kid's lack of issues over personal space, Sam had assumed the guy was used to huggers like him and El, but maybe he wasn't. Sam stepped back awkwardly and cleared his throat. "I don't really have anything planned for today or tomorrow, so why don't I go and get dressed, and then I'll drive you over to the library so you can check the place out? We can hit the grocery store on the way back and pick up whatever you like to eat, plus supplies for the next cooking lesson. How does that sound?"

Sam was pretty sure he'd felt Cameron's hands drag across his hips as he'd stepped back, so maybe Cameron was cool with the hug after all, but the guy continued to stare at him oddly for another few seconds before nodding his assent and stepping away to take his plate to the sink. Sam smiled to himself as Cameron rinsed his dirty dishes and put them into the dishwasher. At least Sam wouldn't have to explain what picking up after yourself meant. That was a good sign, and they could figure the rest out as they went.

"Take it easy, have some more coffee, and I'll be back in fifteen," Sam said as he put his own plate away and headed off to the shower, carefully avoiding getting too close to Cameron as he edged his way out of the kitchen.

# CHAPTER FOUR

WHEN SAM went off to get ready, Cameron wandered into the tiny, closet-sized room next to the kitchen. He guessed it was supposed to be the formal dining room, but it was clear Sam used it mostly as his office. There wasn't much to see, but Cameron was feeling anxious and restless after his talk with Sam… and then there was the hug. Talk about mixed signals. He'd just started getting into it, the warmth and solidity of Sam's chest and the man's strong arms around him, when Sam had pulled back and walked off to get ready to go out, like nothing had happened, leaving him horny and confused.

There was a part of Cameron that was actually relieved Sam wasn't going to jump all over him from day one, like Sean had, but another part was disappointed because it looked like he wasn't going to be getting down to business any time soon either. It would have been nice to get that part out in the open and take the edge off with a little rubbing or even a quick blowjob. Now, he was tense and agitated, wondering why Sam had bothered to hug him in the first place. It was weird.

As he looked out the little window above the desk, a thought suddenly occurred to him, and his stomach twisted. Maybe Sam was one of those guys who liked to take his time and be in control of things. Maybe he liked the chase and he wanted his prey to act all passive and reluctant. Cameron shuddered. He'd had enough experience with that to last a lifetime—with someone who went so slow he hadn't even known what was happening until it was too late. Cameron wasn't sure he could handle it if that was Sam's game. He hated any kind of games, but that wasn't one he'd be able to fake, even if it meant he'd be out on his ass again.

Cameron chewed on his lip rings and stared into the backyard, watching the neat little rows of flowers in their neat little beds sway in the breeze as something else occurred to him. There was a remote possibility Sam was a different kind of animal altogether: a genuinely nice guy who wasn't just in it for what he could get for himself. Cameron wasn't sure he could believe guys like that actually existed outside of a Disney movie. And he sure as hell wasn't going to get suckered in without a hell of a lot of proof, but the little hopeful voice in his head wouldn't let him deny it was possible—not yet.

He really needed to get Sam drunk or high. He wouldn't be able to relax until he'd seen Sam's dark side. Everybody had one. He just needed to know how dark Sam's was so he could figure out how to deal with it.

As he listened to the sounds of Sam puttering around at the back of the house, Cameron lingered over the little office setup, trying to push his messed-up thoughts to the back of his head for the time being. He wasn't going to figure anything out right now, and he didn't want to fuck things up with Sam his first day there. He let his gaze wander over Sam's open laptop, wireless keyboard, and second monitor, before moving on to the wireless printer on top of a little rolling file cabinet next to the desk. It was all very organized and tidy, like the yard, and it seemed like a great place to study. Maybe, if he asked nicely, Sam would let him use it when he was at work.

Cameron could picture himself sitting there, drinking his coffee, and gazing out into the pretty little yard every once in a while as he studied and did whatever else he needed to do to get his life back under control. It was a happy image, and it distracted him enough to let all the other twisted bullshit fade into the background. He'd figure out what Sam's deal was eventually, and he'd do what needed to be done.

"You ready?" Sam asked from the archway into the room, startling him.

The guy was dressed in another pair of boring, ratty khaki cargo shorts, a faded orange Old Navy T-shirt, and brown leather sandals, and

Cameron had to resist the urge to grimace and roll his eyes. Yes, *he* was ready, but it didn't look like Sam was. Someone needed to teach this man how to dress. Cameron wasn't at all surprised there wasn't a boyfriend in the picture if that was what he wore out in public.

Cameron studied Sam a little more closely and decided the guy wasn't a complete wreck. His thick dark hair clung in damp curls against his scalp, and he'd shaved, making him appear younger and almost cute. If only he'd invest in some better clothes, he might actually achieve hotness someday. Cameron considered offering to help with that, but decided to wait until he knew Sam a little better. Besides, if Sam got a boyfriend, it would complicate things, and Cameron needed everything to stay as simple as possible.

"Yeah, I'm ready," Cameron said and followed Sam out to his beat-up sedan. The car surprised him a bit considering how neat and tidy Sam's house was, but he didn't say anything about it. Beggars couldn't be choosers, and Cameron had to remember he was one of the beggars now. He might not be able to afford even a crappy car like this one for a very long time to come, so he might as well get used to it.

The trip to the library actually turned out to be fun. After his confusion and anxiety that morning, Cameron decided to simply take everything Sam said at face value until he knew the man better or could get him drunk. He didn't read anything into Sam's words or actions. He didn't even try to flirt. And, surprisingly, he found himself having a better time than he ever would have thought.

At the library, they quickly located the sections he would need with the help of Amanda, one of the librarians. She was a sweet lady, in her forties maybe, and she seemed more than happy to spend her afternoon helping them find whatever they needed. Sam looked a little surprised at the personal attention they were getting, but Cameron took it in stride. He still didn't understand the effect he had on most women, but he'd gotten used to it. Chris and some of the other guys he used to party with said it was because he was so pretty and older chicks dug pretty boys, but Cameron wasn't sure if that was just Chris trying to give him shit. All he *did* know was he could usually have a woman practically eating out of his hands with only a few shy smiles and a couple of polite words. The only exception to that rule seemed to be his own mother.

Go figure.

Cameron had a ball flirting up a storm with Amanda until it was time to go. He was feeling relaxed and in control for the first time in forever—even if Sam was looking at him like he didn't get him at all—and he was almost bouncing on his feet by the time they made it back to the car.

The grocery store ended up being almost as fun as the library, but in a different way. Walking up and down the aisles with Sam pushing their cart was so weirdly domestic Cameron was actually getting into it. He flirted and laughed with the old lady and her Chihuahua in the produce department, and again with the cashier as they checked out, while Sam followed along with a bemused smile on his face. But this time, it was more about what they were doing together than the attention he was getting from other people. Cameron was almost disappointed when it was time to drive home.

"I think I might leave the grocery shopping to you from now on," Sam said with a laugh as they pulled into his driveway. "You seemed to enjoy it a hell of a lot more than I ever do."

Cameron shrugged and smiled at him as he stepped out of Sam's old clunker and pulled some of the bags out of the back. "It was kind of fun."

"I guess we'll have to see how much fun you think it is a few months from now. By the way, do you have a thing for older women that I should know about?" Sam gave him that curious smile again as he grabbed the bags from his side and headed for the front door to his house.

"God, no. I can't help it if I'm popular with *the ladies*, but I wouldn't even know where to start with girl bits, even if I wanted to." Cameron shuddered dramatically and made his "ick" face, and Sam laughed again. Cameron liked making the man laugh. Sam really was much hotter when he was happy and smiling, enough that Cameron could almost ignore his horrible taste in clothes.

They carried the bags into the kitchen, and Sam showed Cameron where everything went as he put the food away. It would be a while before Cameron remembered it all, but the way Sam was talking, it looked like Cameron was going to have plenty of time in the kitchen to learn.

*Oh joy. Oh rapture.*

The problem was, watching Sam bend and stretch as he put everything in its proper place wasn't helping Cameron remember anything except how horny he was, and he had to excuse himself for a little alone time after the lesson. He realized his first mistake was not jacking off in the shower that morning. He'd been so nervous and in such a hurry to get dressed and looking his best for Sam, he'd sort of skipped that part of his daily routine. Now he seriously needed to take the edge off, if he was going to have more than two brain cells to rub together to keep on his toes and to keep his guard up.

As soon as he made it to his bedroom, Cameron locked the door, climbed onto the futon, and propped himself up on his pillows. He pulled out his iPod and his headphones, cranked up his tunes, and stretched out. He quickly unfastened his belt, popped open the top button of his jeans, and yanked his zipper down, sighing in relief as the tight denim constricting his cock came away and he could rub it through the thin cotton of his boxer briefs. One of the serious drawbacks to wearing tight pants was they became uncomfortable as hell whenever he got a boner, and that was pretty often. How a boy had to suffer for fashion.

Cameron closed his eyes and relaxed against his pillows as he started to stroke himself through his underwear. He let his mind go blank, listening to his masturbation playlist. He rarely thought of anyone in particular when he jacked off. Sometimes he pictured mouths and hands, chests and stomachs, cocks and asses, but not any one person's face or body. Some guys he knew pictured famous people, and he'd tried it once or twice with actors or models he thought were incredibly hot, but most of the time, his fantasies were vague and faceless. He wasn't sure what that said about him, but it certainly never stopped him from getting off.

Cameron pushed his pants and underwear down enough to free his cock, wrapped his hand around it, and then pumped slowly, teasingly, enjoying the cool smoothness of his glass ring as it slid over his heated skin. The ring would heat up soon enough, but he liked the contrast while it lasted.

He swallowed a moan as his hand moved faster up and down his length and he reached down to cup and roll his balls with the other. He was doing this to get off, not put on a show for Sam, so he needed to keep it quiet... *although*, now that he thought about it, maybe he should make some noise. The door was locked, so he wouldn't have any surprise visits, but he could tease a little bit. Cameron wasn't as much of an exhibitionist as Sean had wanted him to be, but he liked getting attention. His rhythm faltered a little as thoughts of Sean threatened to kill his mood, but Cameron shut them down and concentrated on the music and the feel of his hands on his body, imagining Sam standing in the doorway watching and cranking up the volume on the noises he was making.

After a few minutes, he grabbed some lube out of his duffel bag and slicked his dick and his fingers. When he was nice and wet, he drew his knees up close to his chest and started stroking his cock hard, the way he liked it. He squeezed the head before every down-stroke and moaned loudly as he slid a couple of fingers into his ass, teasing and rubbing his gland until he was shivering on the edge. A few more hard pumps on his cock and Cameron cried out as he shot over his stomach and chest.

He lay there for a while afterward, listening to his music and panting, wondering if Sam had heard him and what he was thinking if he had. He started regretting his little performance almost immediately. If Sam really was a nice guy, what would he think of his crazy new houseguest? And if he wasn't, what had Cameron asked for by acting so slutty his first day there?

Sometimes, in moments of deep introspection, it occurred to him how very strange it was that he didn't understand why he did a lot of the things he did. He wasn't stupid, but he did dumb stuff pretty often for a supposedly smart person. With almost four years of intensive therapy after his dad went to jail, he should have a better handle on his behavior. But most of the time, he thought all he'd gotten out of the sessions were wordier labels to give his actions and fancier excuses to explain away why he was the way he was without ever really getting any better. How fucked-up was that?

Cameron rolled his eyes at himself, pulled his headphones off, and sat up. That line of thinking never led anywhere good, and he'd have to face the consequences of his little show sometime. He grabbed the towel he'd used that morning off the back of the only chair in the room and wiped himself down with it. It was still damp and a little cold, but it did the job. He'd wash it with a load of his clothes that night, if Sam would give him another run-through on using the washing machine and dryer… if he didn't kick Cameron out first.

When he was as clean as he was going to get, he pulled his pants and underwear back up, redid his belt, and checked himself out in the mirror above the dresser. His hair was a little messy, but in a good way, so he headed out to find Sam, ready as he was ever going to be to find out what Sam's reaction to his noisy little show was.

Unfortunately, when Cameron finally tracked him down, Sam was out in the backyard, talking to someone over the fence, so Cameron had no way of knowing if the man had even heard any of it or not. He felt like a complete asshole and utterly off-balance as Sam cheerfully introduced him to his neighbor, and then spent the rest of the evening teaching him how to cook BLTs and how to use the washer and dryer again. The man acted completely innocent and oblivious, and Cameron had no idea what to do about it.

At least he actually enjoyed the lessons in domestic stuff, despite his discomfort. He wasn't going to turn into a Little Miss Homemaker, but what he'd done already had made him feel a little more normal, grounded. After the lessons, they sat down for another night on the Xbox and Cameron went to bed cautiously optimistic Sam was almost as good as he seemed—quite possibly vanilla all the way—and that things didn't have to be sick or twisted between them. Cameron was beginning to think, when he did finally get down to business with Sam, he'd be fine with fucking around however Sam wanted to fuck around. Cameron could definitely handle vanilla. It would be a nice change after some of the shit he'd seen and done.

# CHAPTER FIVE

OVER THE next week, Sam thought Cameron settled in quite well. He almost regretted going back to work after his third and final day off. He and Cameron were actually having a pretty good time together cooking, watching movies, playing on the Xbox, and talking about music. Sam had even broken out his dad's guitar for a song or two at Cameron's insistence their third night together, and he'd enjoyed it so much he couldn't remember why he'd stopped playing it for so long.

Oh yeah, Keith had told him he sounded like Bob Dylan when he sang.

As he lay in bed on those nights, the fact that he was having such a good time with Cameron really brought home how lonely he'd been over the last six months. His sister was right. He wasn't made to live alone. With his dad gone, and his *mamá* moved into a retirement community with her friends in Arizona, Sam only had El, her family, and his friends to keep him company, and none of them were there when he woke up in the morning or when he came home from work at night.

Cameron might be a little immature and kind of helpless when it came to the basics of taking care of himself, but he was a good houseguest and a polite and eager student. The guy still seemed to have no concept of personal space, which Sam thought might be part of what had gotten him in trouble in the first place, but Sam was actually looking forward to coming home and finding Cameron there to greet him each night, as corny and 1960s sitcom as that sounded. Maybe when Cameron had finished getting his shit together and was off to a better life, Sam would have to put some serious effort into finding himself a boyfriend again, because he had a strange feeling he was going to be the one with empty-nest syndrome when Cameron finally left.

After his fourth day back at work, Sam came home and the smells of cheese, chilies, cumin, and chili powder enveloped him in a mouthwatering cloud as soon as he opened his front door. Sam had gone over how to make simple chicken enchiladas the day before, and apparently Cameron had decided to give it a shot. Sam set the bag with his dirty jumpsuit and work boots on the floor by the door and wandered over to lean on one of the barstools to watch Cameron putter around his kitchen. Cameron had his headphones on, completely oblivious to his surroundings, and Sam couldn't help but smile. If the kid were only five or six years older, Sam would have been tempted to plant a big kiss right on his lips as a thank you for making his homecoming such a pleasant surprise.

"Hey," he called out loudly enough to be heard over whatever was blaring in the headphones.

Cameron jumped and spun around. When he saw who it was, he pulled the headphones off his ears and let them dangle around his neck. "Hey. Is it that late already?"

Sam didn't come home until almost eight most nights, so it was a little unusual for him to be home before dusk. "I'm a little early. Cesar had everything under control in the shop. He kicked me out of there around ten, and Nina had all the client calls taken care of by lunch, so I got stuck with the paperwork. I can only take so many hours of that before my eyes cross, and I decided to come home. By the smell of that, I'm glad I did."

Cameron's smile was shy, but Sam could tell he was pleased. "I was a little nervous about it, so I started it too soon. I hope it tastes as good as it smells."

"I'm sure it'll be great. So far, you've proven to be a natural. You're going to spoil me," Sam said as he stretched his arms above his head to relieve some of the cramping in his lower back from sitting at his desk all day and then braced his hands on the breakfast bar again.

Cameron's smile changed a little then, his eyes hooded, and his voice dropped almost an octave. "A little spoiling isn't a bad thing. Give me the word, and I'll spoil you any way you want."

Sam rolled his eyes and laughed. "Yeah, yeah, yeah. So you say." He waved a dismissive hand as he walked back the way he'd come, picked up his bag, and headed to his bedroom to get out of his work clothes.

Sam was no longer caught off guard by Cameron's flirting. He'd seen it with the ladies at the library and the grocery store, as well as when he'd introduced Cameron to his eighty-year-old neighbor, Phyllis. The boy couldn't help it, and it had only taken Sam a day or two to figure out he didn't really mean it. Someday, he'd have to have a talk with Cameron about that, because not everyone would understand he wasn't serious. Sam was fine with it, for the time being anyway. He just laughed it off, and then they got back to whatever they'd been talking about before it happened. The kid was sweet and polite and funny most of the time, so Sam forgave anything that was borderline inappropriate.

When he came back out, dressed in his usual comfy shorts and T-shirt, he found Cameron setting plates out on the dining room table. Despite the fact that he was okay with the flirting most of the time, Sam had decided to pull the table out from the wall and have them eat their dinners in there, rather than at the breakfast bar. After their third night together, Cameron's lack of awareness over personal space had made sitting that close to each other a more intimate affair than Sam was comfortable with. He came from a cuddly family, but Cameron could make even *him* uneasy with all the touching, so he'd moved them into the dining room to be safe.

The enchiladas were awesome, as great as all the other meals Cameron had tried so far. The kid was really picking up the cooking lessons fast, and Sam was one stuffed happy camper. He'd have to move up to more complicated recipes soon.

Since Sam was home early enough that night, he decided to take the two of them out for ice cream after dinner to celebrate Cameron's continued success. They got a couple of cones and walked down by the pier for a little people watching. And even though Cameron seemed to be putting a disturbing amount of effort into licking his ice cream cone, Sam spent most of their walk laughing because of Cameron's running fashion police commentary.

"Oh. My. Gawd. What was she thinking?" and "My eyes! My eyes!" were some of his favorites.

Sam actually didn't notice most of the violations until Cameron pointed them out. It was a bit of a learning experience, as well as highly entertaining, and by the time they headed home for some more quality Xbox time, his head was full of enough muffin tops and camel toes and cottage cheese to last a lifetime.

That didn't stop him from having a few beers while Cameron kicked his ass at *Call of Duty* for the umpteenth time. He'd already fallen off the diet wagon for the night, so he figured why the hell not? The beers were enough to get him a little buzzed, but not really drunk, and he was feeling pretty relaxed and more than a little amused as Cameron bounced up and down on the couch, hooting in triumph over Sam's latest spectacular demise. Sam slouched back into the soft cushions and smiled fondly over at him. The kid was definitely pretty, all the more appealing when he didn't realize anyone was looking at him—when he dropped the pretense and just acted natural. Sam would have to point that out to him sometime, when he wasn't humming on a good buzz and about to fall asleep. If only Cameron were four or five years older, Sam might consider....

He kind of lost track of time for a minute, and his attention wandered a little hazily around his living room, until he felt a warm hand sliding up his inner thigh, getting his full attention in a hurry. Cameron was way too close when Sam turned to look at him. The kid's pretty hazel eyes gazed up at him for a few intense seconds before very deliberately dropping to Sam's lap, but it wasn't until Cameron ran his tongue over his lips that anything finally clicked. In that instant, the warning bells registered in Sam's thick head, and he realized Cameron was actually seriously hitting on him and had possibly been serious the whole time.

*Oh shit. I'm an idiot.*

Sam pulled away and scrambled off the couch like he'd been stung. Clearing his throat and trying to look anywhere but at the bulge in the front of Cameron's pants, he said, "Uh, Cameron, what are you doing?"

Cameron leered up at him as he climbed to his knees on the couch and leaned over the arm, arching his back and putting his ass in the air. "Nothing *yet*."

Sam felt his stomach flip, and his buzz got chased away in a hurry by his pounding heart. "Look, I'm sorry if I gave you the wrong impression somewhere, but *this*"—he waved a shaking hand back and forth between the two of them—"isn't going to happen."

Cameron frowned and actually pouted up at him. If the conversation hadn't gone into some really serious territory, Sam might have found the pout kind of cute, but as it was, it only reaffirmed he was in real trouble if he didn't make things clear, right that second.

"Why not? It's just a little fooling around, guys helping each other out, no biggie," Cameron said, looking honestly confused, as if he really couldn't understand why Sam would say no.

Sam moaned. "I don't even know where to start with all the things wrong with what you said." He ran a frustrated hand through his hair and took a few steps away to give himself some more breathing room. "Look, first of all, I'm not really into that kind of thing, meaningless sex, I mean. It *is* a biggie to me. But even if it weren't, and I was only looking for a way to get off, it wouldn't be with you."

Cameron literally flinched back at his words, and Sam swore. "I didn't mean it like that. I only meant, if I were just looking for a hookup, it wouldn't be with someone I lived with, someone who's friends with my sister. You see there's nothing simple about that, right? You see how fucked-up that could get really fast, don't you?"

Cameron stubbornly shook his head. "It doesn't have to get fucked-up. It's just a blowjob. Why does it have to be complicated?"

Sam sighed and rubbed at his now aching head. "Look, Cam. You're here to get your shit together, not to hook up with some older guy you're not even really interested in. El said you had some bad experiences with that already, right? And obviously, it wasn't what you wanted. I get that you're young and horny, but I'm pretty damned sure you could find someone your own age easily enough, someone you might actually like. It doesn't have to be me because I'm *convenient*."

Sam squirmed in the silence that followed and tried again, pleading this time. "I'm sorry, but this isn't going to happen, okay?"

Cameron's expression had gone from confused to wounded, and Sam tried frantically to come up with something else to say that would fix the situation. He didn't want to hurt the kid's feelings. He liked Cameron. And maybe sometimes he even found himself being a little bit attracted to him. But that was weird enough. The thought of actually hooking up with him and taking advantage of someone he knew was vulnerable and struggling with some heavy shit made Sam feel sick to his stomach.

"Cameron, it's not you. There's nothing wrong with you. It's just a bad idea, and I'd rather not mess up what we having going here. We're becoming friends, aren't we?"

Cameron chewed one of his lip rings as his eyes searched Sam's face. Sam had no idea what the kid was thinking because his face had closed off, leaving it void of any expression Sam could put a name to. "Yeah, we're friends."

His voice was dull now, and Sam didn't exactly feel comforted by the words, but he couldn't think of anything else to say that would make things better, so he decided to retreat. "Good. I'm glad. Listen, tomorrow's Saturday, and the shop is always really busy on the weekends, so I need to get some sleep. Are you going to be okay?"

Cameron shrugged. "Yeah. I'll be fine."

"Okay. Good night, Cam."

"Good night."

Sam fled to his bedroom and closed the door with a sigh of relief. It was probably a little cowardly of him not to stay and have a longer conversation with Cameron, but in his defense, Sam didn't have a whole lot of experience with letting guys down easy. Most of the time, he was the one getting the let-down speech, and he couldn't remember a single one of them that had made him feel any better, even when they'd only been about casual sex. Maybe they'd talk some more when he got home from work the next night, if Cameron still seemed upset.

# CHAPTER SIX

CAMERON SHOVED his feet into his purple chucks and pulled the laces so hard one of them snapped. "Shit!" He grabbed the broken ends and knotted them together before tying them as best he could, then headed for the bathroom, grumbling under his breath the whole time. He was frustrated, and angry, and horny. He couldn't believe he'd wasted so much time on buttering Sam up… and for what?

There was a small voice in the back of his head trying to remind him that deep down he'd actually gotten what he'd wanted. He'd tested Sam, and Sam had passed. Sam really was the nice guy he appeared to be. But that voice was currently being drowned out by the sting of rejection, frustration over not getting laid, and bruised pride that a guy like Sam wouldn't even consider a *blowjob* from him.

*WTF?*

So now, he was going out. It was eleven o'clock on a Friday, and he'd been cooped up in that tiny little house, playing domestic goddess, for way too long. He stood in front of the mirror in the bathroom and applied foundation like it was war paint. He kohled his eyes and put on a little mascara and the tiniest hint of glitter. Then he sprayed and flat-ironed his hair until it sat perfectly across his forehead and cheeks. He hadn't dyed it in a while, and the natural mousy-brown roots were starting to show, but the contrast with the black wasn't bad.

He was putting the finishing touches on his outfit—multiple bracelets and a studded purple belt—when he got the text from his friend Chris telling him they were getting close. Chris had been messaging him for weeks, asking where he was, and tonight was the first time Cameron had wanted to respond. He'd only given them the cross street up by the bus stop, because he didn't trust them to know exactly where he was staying yet. He wanted to be able to get away from them if he needed to, and he didn't want any of them knowing about Sam. Cameron wasn't exactly sure why he was being so protective of Sam and Sam's house, especially with the way he was feeling at the moment, but he still couldn't bring himself to give Chris the address.

He stared at the door to Sam's bedroom for a long time before grabbing his jacket, letting himself out of the house, and walking the three blocks down and one block over to the bus stop. Chris drove up a few minutes after he got there, and Brandon and Ken were hanging out the windows yelling at him as the car stopped.

"Hey, man, where the hell have you been?" Ken asked from the passenger seat.

Cameron shrugged. "Around."

"In Long Beach? That ain't around, dude. That's almost off the map. We haven't seen you since that fucked-up night at Sean's. We were worried one of the trolls he invited to your birthday party had gobbled you up." Brandon laughed as he opened the door to the backseat.

Cameron gritted his teeth and rolled his eyes dramatically to hide his sudden queasiness. "As if. The old creeps would have to catch me first."

Everybody laughed, and Cameron squeezed into the backseat, next to Brandon.

"Seriously, dude, that whole scene was fucked-up. Sean didn't tell us it was going to be a PnP with the nursing home set when he invited us. We bugged out not long after you did, but I know some guys who stayed, and they said it turned into an orgy and amateur porn night. It was some crazy shit," Ken said.

"So where are we going?" Cameron asked, desperate to turn the conversation away from "that fucked-up night at Sean's" before he lost his nerve and ran back to Sam's.

"Travis's folks are out of town, so he's having a house party. Figured we'd go there first," Chris said from the driver's seat.

"Free drinks!" Brandon chimed in as he cracked his can of Monster open and downed half of it before offering the can to Cameron.

"If it sucks, we can go out after. Maybe hit the Arena if the vultures don't outnumber us," Chris said as he pulled away from the curb.

"The Arena sucks. Too many high schoolers," Brandon whined.

"Dude, seriously? You graduated what, a year and a half ago?" Ken shot back over his shoulder.

"Shut up, Kenneth. You know I don't go for anything under twenty-five. Any younger and they got no money, unless you count Mommy and Daddy's."

"As someone who's still living on Mommy and Daddy's money, I resemble that remark," Chris laughed.

"If you want someone with his own money, Brandon, you're gonna have to go older than that, around here anyway, unless you find yourself a child star," Ken joked.

"I don't care how old they are, as long as they can keep me in the manner in which I would like to become accustomed," Brandon shot back, and then flipped his hair dramatically.

Listening to his friends give each other shit should have been familiar and comforting, but Cameron felt his stomach twist the more they talked. If he hadn't been so mad and embarrassed over what happened with Sam, he might've told them to let him out and tried to catch the bus home, but he didn't feel like he could go back there yet. He needed the distraction or he'd drive himself crazy.

As they drove to Travis's party, Cam tried to join in the bullshitting, even though his heart wasn't in it. He felt like he was somehow outside of his body, looking down at himself as he laughed and repeated the same old jokes they'd always thrown back and forth. He wasn't feeling it, but maybe after a few drinks and some messing around with someone hot and willing, he'd be able to get out of his funk and enjoy himself again. Hell, if he couldn't find anyone decent enough at the party, one of the three knuckleheads in the car would do, if he got desperate. They'd all fucked around with each other a few times, at least when they got trashed enough. Cameron wasn't sure he wanted to get completely wasted but was self-aware enough to know it would probably happen anyway, now he'd finally agreed to go out with them again.

# CHAPTER SEVEN

SAM'S ALARM went off *way* too early the next morning. It had taken him a long time to fall asleep, even with the benefit of a couple of beers in his system, and he'd woken up several times during the night. He'd probably only gotten about three or four good hours of sleep by the time 5:00 a.m. rolled around, and he was running mostly on autopilot as he stumbled into the shower.

He was still only partially awake after his shower, so it took him a good minute or two to understand what he was seeing in the bathroom, now that his eyes were open. There were black streaks, glitter, and powder all over the sink. Makeup containers, a hair product bottle, and Cameron's flat iron were resting on the counter, the cord still plugged into the wall. The mirror had some sort of residue spritzed all over it, and there was a damp towel on the floor.

The last of his grogginess faded pretty fast as he took it all in. He wanted to storm into Cameron's bedroom and demand to know what was going on but decided he probably shouldn't do that while he was only wearing a towel, particularly after their conversation the night before. He dried off and got dressed quickly and *then* stomped down the hall to Cameron's room.

He banged on the door. "Cameron!" When no one answered, he pounded on the door again. When there was still no reply, he opened the door and switched on the light. The room was a wreck, like the bathroom, clothes strewn all over the floor, Cameron's various beauty

46

and hair care products tumbled out onto the bed, the empty bag he usually kept them in tossed on the floor.

"What the hell?"

As Sam tried to get his brain wrapped around the disaster that had been a reasonably clean and tidy room only the day before, he heard the front door open and close, so he turned and headed back into the hall, only to have an obviously drunk and bedraggled Cameron run right into him.

"Jesus, Cameron. Have you been out all night?" Sam asked as he struggled to right the two of them. The smells of booze and clove cigarettes rolled over him in a wave of unpleasantness.

Cameron put a hand on the wall to steady himself and blinked blearily up at Sam. "I guess. I—" Whatever else he was going to say was cut off as he slapped a hand to his mouth, his eyes bugged out, and he pushed past Sam, running for the bathroom.

Sam hurried after him, feeling pissed off and concerned in equal measures. He found Cameron where he expected, kneeling in front of the toilet and coughing into the bowl. Sam shook his head as he dug out a washcloth and wet it in the sink. When Cameron came up for air, he handed it over and watched as the kid used it to wipe his face. Sam stayed with him and flushed the toilet in between Cameron's bouts of retching, because he knew he was a sympathy puker, and he really didn't want to get that cycle started between the two of them. The sounds were bad enough without the visual making it worse.

When it looked like Cameron was finally done, Sam helped him to his feet and half carried him back to his room. Cameron groaned when Sam dumped him on his bed but was otherwise silent.

"Are you going to be okay?" Sam asked.

Cameron swallowed and nodded. Sam rolled his eyes and went to the kitchen to get a glass of water and some Tylenol.

"Here. Take these and drink all of it," he said as he handed the pills and glass over. He grabbed the trashcan from the corner of the room to leave by the bed. "I suggest you sleep on your stomach or your side and use this if you feel sick again. Did you take anything other than alcohol?"

Cameron opened his eyes a little and glared at him. "No." His voice was raspy but still managed to be petulant.

Sam glared right back. "You're a mess. I wasn't exactly reaching with the question."

"I didn't, okay? I just had too much to drink. I forgot how long it's been since I partied. I'll be fine."

Cameron's voice had gotten distinctly whiney, and Sam decided to let any more questions wait until the kid sobered up. "Fine. I'll go get you another glass of water, in case you want it later."

He went to the bathroom and refilled the glass. When he got back to the room, Cameron was out cold, sleeping on his side with the trashcan right below him. Sam set the glass down on a small shelf by the bed, pulled the curtains over the windows, and closed the door softly behind him as he left. After calling the shop to let Nina know he was going to be a little late, Sam poured a cup of coffee and walked out to the porch to give himself a chance to relax and let his irritation fade.

After his second cup, he was feeling much more sympathetic. This was the first time Cameron had left any kind of mess in the house, so it really wasn't that big of a deal. And even though the kid wasn't legal to drink, Sam had had more than his fair share of hangovers before his twenty-first birthday, so he couldn't really cast any stones there either. He wasn't angry anymore, but he was a little worried and guilty. Elena had said Cameron was trying to get away from all of that bullshit, and after only one disagreement between the two of them, the kid was out all night, getting plastered, and doing who knows what else. Maybe it was his fault for being so blind and letting things get far enough Cameron's feelings got hurt. He should have been paying more attention.

Before Sam finally left for work, he checked on Cameron a couple more times. The kid was sleeping pretty soundly, and he looked like he was over the worst of it, so Sam left the bottle of Tylenol next to the glass of water and headed off to the shop. He sent a text to Elena, asking her to check on Cameron that afternoon, if she had time, and then the garage was so slammed he really didn't have much of a chance to think about the kid until it was time to head home.

Sam was a little concerned when he walked in the door at eight and all the lights were out in the house and no dinner was waiting on the counter. They'd decided the Saturdays he worked would always be Cameron's night to cook, because Sam was usually so beat by the time he got home he could barely keep his eyes open.

He set his bag down, went to Cameron's door, and knocked quietly. "Cameron? You okay?" When he didn't get a response, Sam opened the door to find Cameron sprawled out on his bed with his laptop propped on his chest as he madly typed on his keyboard.

"Hey! You okay?" Sam tried a little louder this time because Cameron had his headphones on. Cameron barely glanced at him before holding up his index finger in the universal "give me a sec" gesture. Irritated, Sam crossed his arms over his chest and leaned against the doorjamb to wait, his frown deepening with every second as the little shit appeared to be finishing a game.

"Sorry, I was almost done." Cameron didn't sound particularly sorry, but Sam decided to let it go in lieu of a more pressing matter.

"Where's dinner?"

Cameron's pretty hazel eyes went wide, but Sam wasn't convinced the surprise was genuine. "Is it my night? I'm sorry, I forgot."

"You forgot?"

Sam's disbelief was probably even more obvious than Cameron's faux surprise, because the kid got defensive in a hurry. "Yeah. People do forget things sometimes, Sam. We aren't all perfect."

Sam frowned even harder. "What's that supposed to mean?"

Cameron's lower lip pouted out, making the balls on his lip rings catch the light from his laptop screen as he turned his head away. "Look. I said I was sorry. I forgot. That's all. Can't we order pizza or something?"

Sam took a deep breath and let it out slowly so he wouldn't say anything he'd regret later. "Fine. I'll order pizza. But you're on for tomorrow night *and* Monday night, since you skipped tonight. And for future reference, a hangover isn't a valid excuse for not doing your job. You might want to remember that when you're out in the real world."

Cameron's lips tightened unattractively, but he didn't say anything, and Sam decided to walk away. As he headed back toward the kitchen, he yelled, "And if you haven't cleaned the bathroom already, I suggest you do so before the pizza gets here."

The sound of stomping feet making their way through the back of the house let him know Cameron wasn't going to ignore him at least.

"Twenty years old, my ass," he mumbled to himself as he pulled a beer out of the fridge and went to find the number for delivery. "I'm living with a fucking twelve-year-old."

After calling in the order, Sam collapsed onto his couch and stared at the empty black surface of his flat screen. He heard water running, off and on, as he sat there and sipped his beer, and he wondered again what the hell Elena had gotten him into. He'd thought he had a decent idea of who was staying with him, but the Cameron he saw today was nothing like the one he'd been living with for the past week and a half, and he didn't like this version at all. Sam dropped his head against the back of the couch and closed his eyes. He really hoped "bratty Cameron" didn't hang around for long, because he had no idea how to handle him.

As he sat there with his eyes closed, a thought occurred to him and he smiled, despite the crappiness of his homecoming. He wondered if this was some sort of payback from his sister for all the years of misery and brattitude he'd put her through growing up. Maybe she knew exactly how much of a shit Cameron could be, and was home, at that very moment, laughing her butt off at her brother's expense. He could almost picture her cackling, "Payback's a bitch, baby brother."

It was a definite possibility, but Sam thought it was probably more likely Cameron's feelings were hurt over what happened the night before, and he was too young and immature to know how to express it. Either way, Sam didn't have the energy to deal with it after a Saturday at the shop, so he was relieved when Cameron only came out to get his pizza and went straight back to his room for the rest of the night, without much more than a mumbled thanks for dinner. At least the bathroom was clean when Sam headed off to bed a few hours later. He'd have to take that as a win until he figured out what the hell he was supposed to do now.

# CHAPTER EIGHT

CAMERON DIDN'T sleep well that night. The thoughts and feelings he'd been trying to avoid all day wouldn't let him. He tried to play *Lego Star Wars* again, but even that didn't help. His brain wasn't letting him hide from the simple fact that he didn't feel any better now than he had before he'd gone out with his friends. In fact, he felt worse, *much* worse.

He could almost hear Dr. Wingate's voice. *"Do you feel you learned anything from the experience?"*

*Yeah, I fucking learned I puke all over myself and feel like I'm dying when I mix vodka, tequila, and cloves.*

*"Was that what you were hoping to learn?"*

Cameron groaned and pulled his pillow over his head, hugging it close to his face. *No*, that was not what he'd been hoping for. He'd wanted a distraction, a way to blow off a little steam and maybe get laid. But things got out of hand fast, like they always did when he went out in a bad mood.

Who was he kidding? Things got out of hand just as fast when he was in a good mood too. And now he'd fucked things up with Sam, not permanently, judging by the fact Sam hadn't kicked him out and had actually bought him dinner, but he *had* fucked up, *again*. And now Sam probably thought he was not only a loser and a slut, but a party boy and a tweaker too.

Cameron didn't remember everything from the night before or that morning, but he did remember Sam practically holding his hair while he puked in the toilet and then tucking him in bed and getting him meds and water for the hangover. Sam actually took care of him, and all Cameron did to thank him was act like a shit. He'd managed to stay mad at Sam all day, but he couldn't do it anymore. Guilt and shame clawed at him, and Cameron squeezed the pillow tighter to his face, moaning even louder this time and cringing inwardly.

He had to apologize, *really* apologize, but he didn't know how.

If he'd still been with Sean, his apology would've involved an "I'm sorry" blowjob, at the very least, but he knew that wasn't an option now. So how the hell was he supposed to make it up to him?

"Sam's a nice guy."

Cameron said it once, into the pillow, and then again into the dark of his room after shoving the pillow away.

"Sam is a *nice* guy."

A part of him knew how sad it was that statement seemed like such a revelation, but there was no denying it. Sam was simply a normal, *nice* guy, trying to live his life and giving Cameron a chance to do the same, without expecting anything in return. If Sam were Elena, Cameron would have groveled, and flirted, and given her the puppy dog eyes, until she forgave him. But he'd pretty much burned that bridge to the ground with Sam. Now he had to come up with something else.

The answer, when it came to him, was so simple and obvious Cameron felt stupid for agonizing over it for so long. He'd like to blame it on how tired and hungover he was, but really, he was just fucked-up. With his parents and the people he hung out with, it didn't take a genius to figure that one out.

THE NEXT morning, the alarm on Cameron's phone went off at seven, and he actually got up without hitting snooze even once. After his shower, he didn't bother to straighten his hair or put in his contacts. He didn't put on any foundation or one of his usual outfits. He simply pulled on a clean pair of pajama bottoms and a loose T-shirt, grabbed his glasses, and went to the kitchen to get breakfast started.

Sam had told him his shop didn't open until later on Sundays, so the man wouldn't have to be up before the crack of dawn, like he usually was. But Sam also didn't seem to grasp the meaning of the phrase sleeping in, so Cameron didn't have time to try anything new or fancy for breakfast. He'd have to stick to something he knew: eggs, bacon, and toast.

By the time Sam wandered into the kitchen, Cameron had everything cooked and already plated. He'd even found a melon in the refrigerator and sliced it up on the side, like he'd seen the chefs on TV do.

Sam seemed confused as he glanced back and forth between the plates of food and Cameron. But confused was a hell of a lot better than pissed off, and Cameron smiled tentatively back.

"Your hair's curly."

Whatever Cameron had been expecting Sam to say, that wasn't it, but he shrugged and took it as the opening it was.

"I didn't use the flat iron this morning."

"And you have glasses," Sam said, and then he shook his head as if to clear it. "Sorry. I just haven't seen you like this before. It's nice."

Cameron rolled his eyes. He looked like shit, and he knew it. Instead of saying it, though, he pushed the plate at Sam across the breakfast bar. "This is going to get cold. I'll get your coffee."

Sam gave him a bemused look but took the plate anyway and carried it into the dining room. Cameron pulled a mug out of the cabinet and filled it, put one spoonful of sugar and a tiny bit of milk in it, the way he'd seen Sam make it, and then carried the mug with him to the dining room along with his own breakfast.

"Thanks," Sam said as he took the mug and sipped at it, watching Cameron like he was afraid he was going to grow another head or something. "This is good," Sam finally said into the silence that followed, and Cameron smiled.

Gathering up his courage, he took a deep breath and plunged on, addressing the elephant in the room. "Thanks. I figure I owed you at least this much after yesterday... and the day before." He chewed on his lip ring as he watched Sam set his fork down and regard him seriously for a minute.

"You could say I was a little surprised by the last couple of days... and not in a good way."

"I'm sorry, Sam."

Sam sighed and rubbed between his eyes. "Me too, Cameron. I didn't mean to hurt your feelings. I probably could have handled things better. I like to think I would have, if I'd been sober, but the truth is, there's no guarantee on that. I never said I was perfect either."

Cameron shook his head. "I was stupid."

"Look, I like you, Cameron. From what I've seen over the last week or so, I think you're a good person who's hit a rough patch. I want to help you, for Elena's sake, as well as your own. And I want us to be friends, without any of that other bullshit to complicate things. Can we do that?"

Cameron nodded. "Yeah, I'd like that."

Sam blew out a breath and relaxed back into his chair. "Good. Then we'll forget the last couple of days even happened and get back to how we were before... only maybe tone the flirting down a bit, okay?"

Cameron laughed uncomfortably. "Yeah, okay."

He watched Sam out of the corner of his eye as the man happily gobbled up his breakfast, and Cameron felt like he'd leveled up in their relationship. Project "nice guy," or "be like Sam," had taken off to a good start. All he had to do now was keep his promises to Sam and to himself, and the next few months would be cake. Sam already thought he was a good person under all the bullshit and that helped. When people only thought the worst of you, it was easy to prove them right. Cameron hoped the same was true for the opposite. Maybe if he pretended Sam was a more butch version of Elena, he could manage to avoid fucking up again as long as they lived together.

That was the plan he decided on anyway.

Unfortunately for Cameron, Sam wasn't Elena. And pretending he was got more and more difficult as the next few weeks went by. Cameron kept his promises. He continued to do his nice guy routine, cleaning up after himself, cooking his assigned meals, and studying when he was supposed to be studying. And he didn't go out and party with his friends or flirt with Sam at all, no matter how much he wanted to. But as each day passed, it got harder and harder to be around Sam and *not* want things he couldn't have.

The problem was, the more time he spent with Sam, the more he liked him, *really* liked him. They spent almost every night together unless Sam had a class or he was working late. They ate together. They played video games. They watched movies and listened to music. Sam even gave him a few lessons on his dad's guitar. Sam was kind and patient and funny. Even when he was tired and a little grumpy, he was never really nasty. It was all so sweet, and normal, and perfect—how was anyone *not* supposed to fall for a guy like that?

Eventually, it got to the point where Cameron couldn't even remember why he'd thought Sam wasn't his type. Okay sure, if he really sat down and thought about it, he could remember thinking Sam was too old and sort of plain and goofy, but that wasn't what he saw when he looked at him now. He saw a great guy with a nice face, hot body, and the warmest, deepest brown eyes ever… and it was killing him that Sam was only a couple of feet away from him all night, every night, and he couldn't do anything about it, without fucking up what they already had.

It was so unfair.

But he didn't flirt. He didn't try to touch Sam or push for anything to happen between them. He continued to be a good boy. He was actually pretty proud of himself. He thought Dr. Wingate might have been proud of him too, for "*managing his impulses and remaining cognizant of the ramifications of his actions.*" Cameron was actually feeling pretty damned good about himself.

# CHAPTER NINE

SAM CLOSED his eyes and dropped his head back on the headrest in the backseat of Ryan's car, enjoying the breeze coming from the open window. He had no idea where his friends were taking him, but it was kind of nice not to be in charge for a little while. That afternoon, Ryan and his partner, John, had ambushed him at work, saying they were staging an intervention and demanding he take a long lunch with them, or else. Sam wasn't sure what the "or else" would have entailed, but they didn't have to twist his arm. He'd just been really busy with work and helping Cameron settle in, so he hadn't felt like accepting any of their recent invitations. He wasn't hiding. He was simply enjoying hanging out at home these days, and he didn't feel a pressing need to go out.

"You're not falling asleep on us are you?" Ryan called from the driver's seat. "I told you we should have staged this intervention sooner. Look at him. He's worn out."

Sam chuckled and cracked open one eye. Ryan was staring at him in the rearview mirror with genuine concern. "I'm fine. I just stayed up a little late last night. I got *Diablo III* on my way home from work yesterday and decided I couldn't wait to crack it open."

"*Diablo III?*" Ryan asked.

"Video game, honey," John answered for him, patting his lover's shoulder.

Ryan rolled his eyes. "Gawd. We definitely should have staged the intervention sooner."

"Ha, ha, ha," Sam said as he pushed himself upright. "It was a work night. It wasn't as if I would have been going out partying anyway. And we had a good time, which is why I'm paying for staying up so late now."

"We?" Ryan asked, drawing out the word suggestively.

"Cameron and I."

"Oh." Ryan's voice couldn't have sounded more disappointed and disapproving if he'd tried.

"That's the kid who's staying with you, right?" John asked.

"Yes." Sam really didn't want to go over this particular topic again. He'd already gotten the "what the fuck are you doing taking some strange club kid into your house" speech over the phone from Ryan, and he wasn't in the mood to defend himself or Cameron yet again.

"Sam—" Ryan started, but John cut him off.

"Look, there's Joe Jost's. Why don't we wait and talk when we're inside?"

Ryan held his tongue, and Sam smiled at John. The man always seemed to know when to cut in before Ryan really pissed someone off. Sam and Ryan had been friends since high school, but he had to admit, he liked Ryan so much better now he and John were together. John kept his partner's dickishness to a manageable level.

"Look, we're worried about you, okay?" Ryan started, as soon as the waiter dropped off their drinks and took their lunch orders.

"I'm fine. Everything's fine. The shop is doing great. Cesar is working out perfectly, like I knew he would, so I'll have more free time to come and see you guys from now on. I promise."

"Does that mean you'll actually say yes the next time we invite you out?" Ryan's thin black eyebrows arched high over the lenses of his frameless glasses, and he cocked his head dramatically to the side.

"I'll do my best, but you know Saturdays are our busiest days. I didn't want to leave Cesar by himself until he felt comfortable, and you know how tired I am after working one. Even if I came to your party last month, I probably would've passed out on your couch an hour after I got there."

"That's fine with us. We would have found someone cute to tuck you in one of the guest rooms and made you breakfast in the morning," Ryan said, winking at him, and Sam rolled his eyes.

Another reason he hadn't taken them up on most of their invitations was because, ever since Keith left him, they'd been on a manhunt for him, and up until recently, Sam hadn't been quite ready for that. He still wasn't completely sure he was ready for whomever *Ryan* came up with, but in the last few weeks, he'd thought maybe it was time to start trying again. Watching the two lovebirds across from him now, as they exchanged tender touches and wordless communications with each other only made him realize it more.

Sam missed that. More than the sex and the passion, he missed the connection that came with a long-time lover, a partner, and he really wanted to have it again.

Before Sam could get too morose, the waiter brought their sandwiches and another round of drinks, and they were all quiet for a few minutes while they ate.

"It isn't just that we're worried about you, Sam. We miss you too," John said, brushing his thick, wavy blond hair out of his eyes and glancing at Ryan briefly before putting his hand on Sam's arm. "It seems like forever since we've seen you, actually face-to-face."

"I know. I missed you guys too." Sam patted his hand gently, and John withdrew it after a few seconds, while Ryan smiled fondly at the two of them.

It had taken years before Ryan would allow even that much contact between his boyfriend and any other man without turning into a jealous prick, and Sam was relieved to discover no ground had been lost in that respect. He'd been a little worried, since Keith had dumped him and put him back on the market, that Ryan might turn into a possessive freak again.

"Look, enough of the mushiness. Let's get to the real reason we called you out here," Ryan broke in on his thoughts, and Sam tensed, readying himself for another lecture. "Relax, Sam. I'm not going to hassle you on your live-in charity case again, at least not right now. I'm talking about your birthday, the big three-O, that precious moment where you teeter on the pinnacle only to start the slow downward slide into middle age. We haven't forgotten it's coming up."

Sam relaxed a little in the middle of his speech but grimaced and threw his napkin at Ryan when he reached the end. "Yeah, I haven't forgotten that either."

John smiled sympathetically and patted Sam's arm again. "Sweetie, it's okay. It happens to us all, eventually."

"Thanks. I feel so much better."

"Seriously, Sam, we're not going to let this one slip by like the last one," Ryan said, his dark-blue eyes serious and his pointy chin pushed out stubbornly.

Sam's twenty-ninth birthday had been a bit of a bust. He'd gone out of town with Keith, rather than letting his friends throw him a party at home, and they'd ended up fighting for half the weekend over Keith's drunken groping of every male body he came in contact with on their club-crawl. Looking back, Sam should have taken that as a sign of things to come, but he hadn't wanted to admit it then.

"Okay, okay. You're right. I don't want that either."

"We've also decided that we're having it at your place, so you can't back out at the last minute, even if you wanted to," Ryan continued.

"You have, have you?" Sam laughed.

"Yes, we have. And you're not allowed to argue. Don't worry about the food and decorations. We'll bring all that. And I'm sure Felix and Jeremy could be prevailed upon to supply the wine. We'll figure out who else we can get to take care of the rest. All you have to do is be there to let us in and have the place as neat and clean as it always is."

"I think I can manage that."

"Good. Do you think your twink can manage to make himself scarce for one night?" Ryan asked.

Sam frowned. Up until the last question, he was feeling all touched and warm and fuzzy that his friends were willing to do so much for him. "His name is Cameron, and I consider him a friend. I'm not going to exclude him from my birthday party, especially not when he lives there."

Ryan opened his mouth, but John stopped him with a hand on his arm. "That's fine, Sam. It's your house and your party. We'll look forward to meeting him. Won't we, Ryan?"

Sam saw John's fingers tighten on his lover's arm, and Ryan stopped stroking his soul patch long enough to let out an irritated sigh and roll his eyes. "Fine. It's your birthday. But I'm not responsible if the kid gets drunk and child services shows up."

Sam was about to come back with something equally bitchy, when he reminded himself he'd thought something similar the day Elena had first showed up at his door with Cameron. "He's twenty, Ryan. Child services isn't going to show up. Just be nice to him, okay? For me? Please?"

Ryan snorted. "Okay. I'll be nice to him. Now, let's talk details. When do you want it, and who do you want there, other than our usual crew?"

Luckily for Sam, his birthday was actually on a Saturday, and there would be no way Cesar would let him work on his thirtieth birthday, so he could give them a definite date. They hashed out a few more details, but John insisted they wanted to do this for him, so they didn't really ask him to weigh in on much more than the basics. After lunch, they drove him back to the shop, and both Ryan and John gave him a big hug before heading back to their offices. Sam went back to work actually feeling pretty good about his upcoming introduction into the thirty and over years.

His good mood lasted throughout the day and only got better when he opened the door to his house that night and smelled something incredible coming from the kitchen. He headed straight for it, after dropping his bag by the door, and was greeted with the sight of Cameron dancing around his kitchen in another pair of too tight, low-slung, skinny jeans and a wife-beater so thin it was almost transparent. Sam had opened his mouth to comment on how great everything smelled, but no words escaped as he stood there watching Cameron twist and roll his hips to the beat barely audible from his headphones. Cameron was humming along to the music as he alternated between sautéing mushrooms in a pan and stirring something in one of Sam's pots, and Sam simply stood there, frozen in place with his mouth hanging open.

Luckily for him, Cameron turned around before Sam had time to figure out exactly what he was feeling or thinking because he wasn't sure his conscience really wanted to know.

"Hey! You're home early again," Cameron said as he pulled off the headphones and moved the pan of mushrooms off the burner.

"Uh. I didn't know you had tattoos," Sam replied stupidly.

Cameron blinked at him a couple of times and then shrugged. "Yeah, I started right after I turned eighteen," he said, looking down at himself for a second before smiling back up at Sam. "Can't ever have just one, right?"

This was the first time Sam had seen Cameron without a shirt on, or in a shirt that was so thin it might as well not be there, and there were several tattoos on his torso, including a giant one of a phoenix across his shoulder blades that must have cost a fortune. There was also a set of steel bars in Cameron's nipples to go with the belly stud Sam had already seen. He cleared his throat and shifted a little uncomfortably. "I've only got a couple. The sun on my arm, obviously, and there's a guitar on my shoulder for my dad. Nothing as impressive as yours."

Cameron shrugged again. "I had to go back four times for the phoenix. But it was kind of important to me." He turned back to the stove to stir whatever was in the pot and didn't elaborate.

Sam was still feeling a little unsettled, so he didn't push, even though he was curious. "I'm going to go get changed, but I wanted to tell you whatever that is smells wonderful."

Cameron smiled over his shoulder. "Thanks."

Cameron wasn't wearing his glasses, so it was easy to see all the different colors and the warmth in his hazel eyes. He hadn't straightened his hair either, and it curled softly around his face and neck. If only the kid were three or four years older, Sam might have been tempted to plant a kiss right where one of those curls teased his nape, but instead, he returned the smile and retreated quickly to his bedroom to change out of his work clothes.

Dinner turned out to be the best mushroom lasagna Sam had ever had, from a recipe Cameron had found online. Sam had started leaving cash for Cameron so he could take the bus to the grocery store if there were things he needed, and Cameron had started surprising him with more and more adventurous meals. Cameron wasn't always successful with everything he tried, but Sam did his best to be supportive, and most of the time, like tonight, it paid off.

"This is incredible, Cam. Thank you," he said as he leaned back in his chair and considered undoing the top button on his shorts.

Since they'd had their little disagreement and subsequent talk about boundaries, they'd actually started taking more meals together at the breakfast bar and on the couch, rather than the table. But Cameron still seemed to like doing the whole formal dining setup at the table when he made a real effort at dinner, and Sam didn't mind. He thought it was kind of sweet, actually. His dining room wasn't big enough to have the table out, with all the leaves in it and all six chairs around it, very often, but with just the two of them, there was still enough room to keep his office setup and the table out at the same time, if only barely.

"Thanks," Cameron said. "I figured it was a lot of work, but the steps themselves seemed easy, so I thought I could manage it without screwing up too badly, and I wanted to celebrate a little."

Sam looked up from contemplating how much he would pay later if he scooped another serving onto his plate. "Celebrate?"

Cameron chewed his lip ring and gave him a shy smile. "I took another practice test today, and I did really good on it. I'm going to go over it with Elena the next time she comes, but I think I might be ready to sign up for a testing date."

"That's awesome, Cameron! I'm sure you'll do great on it."

"I hope so. Even if I pass, it's only the beginning of everything I have to do, but it'll help. I'm sorry I haven't had much luck finding a job yet."

Sam shook his head. "Don't worry about it. You're not really costing me that much more than if I was on my own anyway, and we can figure something out after you get a job and start making enough to get back on your feet. Really, it's no big deal."

"Okay, cool. Are you done?" Cameron asked as he stood up and gathered his plate.

"Yeah." Sam sighed and gave up on any thoughts of cramming anything more into his already full stomach. "But I'll get this. You did the hard part. I can clean up."

Sam took both their plates from Cameron and headed for the kitchen, but Cameron followed a moment later with the tray of lasagna. Thankfully, the kid had put on another shirt while Sam had changed, so Sam no longer had to suffer through that weird unsettled feeling he'd had earlier. Cameron with no nipple studs or tattoos was a lot less distracting.

"Are you sure you don't want me to help? I made a big mess," Cameron said as he set the casserole dish on the bar and went back for their glasses.

"I can see that," Sam said, laughing as he looked over all the pots, pans, and bowls on his counters. "Don't worry about it. There isn't enough room for two people in here anyway. If I get tired, I'll let you know."

Earlier, Sam had talked Cameron into a game of *Guitar Hero*—another game he'd bought recently—instead of letting Cameron clean up while the lasagna baked, so really, it was his own fault the kitchen was still a mess.

It actually didn't take Sam long to clean up, but Cameron was already asleep on the couch by the time he finished, passed out cold with Sam's Nook on his chest. The Nook had been a Christmas present from Sam's *mamá*, even though Sam hadn't exactly had much time to read in recent years. He'd tried, but most nights after work, he'd only get through a couple of pages before he fell asleep, and then he'd have to read the same pages over again the next night, so it took him forever to finish anything. But Cameron loved to read and had gotten more use out of the thing in the past few weeks than Sam ever had. Sam was considering giving it to the kid as a reward when he passed his GED or got his first job.

Sam sat on the arm of the couch and looked down at Cameron as he slept. The kid really was exceptionally pretty, with his delicate cheekbones, arched eyebrows, perfectly straight little nose with a dimple in the end, and sculpted, slightly pouty lips. Occasionally, Sam wondered what it would feel like to kiss someone with rings in his lips. He'd gone out with a guy who had a ring in his eyebrow once but never anyone with snakebites. Would it add to the experience or would you have to be careful how you kissed so you wouldn't tug on them too hard or chip a tooth?

Sam was saved from his pointless train of thought when Cameron's eyes opened and he gave him a sleepy smile. Sam cleared his throat and looked away, embarrassed to be caught staring while the guy was asleep. "Hey. Did you go out partying last night and I missed the walk of shame this morning?" he joked.

Cameron rolled his eyes and sat up. "No. I guess I didn't sleep well after we finished the game."

"Anything I can do to help?"

"No. It's okay. It happens sometimes."

Sam wasn't sure what that meant, but he got the impression Cameron was uncomfortable with the topic, which of course made him even more curious, but he let it go. "You want to kick my ass at *Guitar Hero* again for an hour or so?"

Cameron chuckled and shook his head. "I'm sleepy enough you just might beat me this time, but I think I should go to bed."

Sam was a little disappointed. He'd had a pretty great day, and he didn't want it to end. But he hadn't gotten much sleep the night before either because of how late they'd stayed up, and unlike Cameron, he couldn't sleep in the next day, so all he said was "Okay, good night."

"Good night."

As Cameron picked up the Nook and headed to the back of the house, Sam called out to him, "Hey, Cameron, before I forget, I had lunch with a couple of my friends this afternoon, Ryan and John, I told you about them. They're going to throw a birthday party for me here a week from Saturday. I wanted to give you a heads-up."

Cameron turned and looked at him. After a few seconds of chewing on his lip ring—always the one on the right for some reason—he asked, "It's your birthday?"

"On that Saturday, yeah." He avoided mentioning it was his big three-O. He wasn't sure why.

"Does that mean I'm invited?"

Sam snorted. "Of course you're invited. Don't be stupid."

Cameron gave him an oddly shy smile. "Okay, cool. Is there anything I can do to help out?"

"They said they wanted to do this for me. I figured I'd go to the shop or to the beach or something so I won't be in the way. If you really want to help, we can ask them when they get here."

"Cool. I can do that."

"See you tomorrow. I hope you sleep better tonight."

"Thanks. See you tomorrow."

Sam spent another couple of hours trying to get caught up on some of the TV shows he had on DVR and finally gave up and went to bed after he had to keep replaying parts because he fell asleep. As he curled up under the sheets, he smiled to himself. This birthday was going to be great. He just knew it.

# CHAPTER TEN

ON THE day of the party, Cameron woke up feeling really excited, despite how nervous he was about meeting pretty much *all* of Sam's friends at the same time. Since his last disastrous night out, Cameron actually hadn't left the house except once or twice when Sam or Elena took him to a restaurant and his trips to the library or the grocery store. After all that time alone, he was dying for a bit of social interaction. He was well aware he wouldn't know anyone at the party, other than Elena and her family, but he was feeling pretty optimistic he'd be able to make some new friends, grown-up friends he and Sam could have in common.

He took extra time in the bathroom that morning, straightening his hair, putting on foundation, and smudging a tiny bit of kohl around his eyes. He wasn't going clubbing so he didn't want to overdo it, but he wanted to look his best for Sam's friends. It took him forever to finally decide on what to wear. He still hadn't been back to his mom's house to get any more of his things, if they hadn't been trashed already, so his selection was somewhat limited. But that didn't stop him from trying on everything he had before settling on the skinny jeans he'd been wearing when he first met Sam and the green polo that made his eyes look more green than brown.

Of course, then he had to spend another half hour picking up the mess he'd made in his bedroom, so it was as tidy as it could be for the party. He had a feeling Sam's party wasn't going to be as wild as he was used to, but he didn't know that for sure, so it was better to be safe than sorry. He didn't plan on taking anyone back to his room, but he couldn't guarantee someone else wouldn't as the night wore on, and he didn't want Sam's friends thinking he was a slob.

When he finally emerged, he heard Sam laughing at him from the kitchen. "Sure you don't need some more time in the bathroom before I take my shower?"

Cameron grinned sheepishly as he climbed onto one of the stools at the breakfast bar. "Sorry. You weren't waiting too long, were you? I've been in my room for the past hour."

"No. I'm just giving you shit. I had some breakfast and a nice lazy sit on the back porch while you were primping."

Cameron stuck out his tongue, and Sam chuckled as he put his plate and mug in the dishwasher and closed the door. Sam patted him on the top of the head as he passed on his way to the shower. "I like the curly better, but I'm flattered you got dressed up for my party. Now, if *I'm* not back in a half hour, call 911 because you'll know something's gone terribly wrong."

"Ha. Ha. Ha," Cameron said, watching with sad eyes as Sam walked away. He didn't bother to hide his feelings because he knew Sam couldn't see him.

His unrequited desire for the man hadn't diminished. If anything, his feelings had only gotten stronger. But Sam still treated him like an annoying younger brother most of the time, and Cameron was too scared to mess up what they had by making another play for him. He kept thinking maybe once he'd gotten his GED and had a job, Sam might start seeing him as something other than a dumb kid. He'd been pushing himself hard, studying and filling out job applications. But late June seemed to be a bad time to try to get a job, and even though he was only a couple of weeks away from the testing date he'd signed up for, it still didn't make seeing Sam every day any easier. Maybe tonight he could make some progress in that area. If he could win over some of Sam's friends, it might make Sam look at him a little differently. It was worth a shot anyway.

True to his word, Sam came out less than a half hour later, dressed in his usual outfit of cargo shorts and a T-shirt, and Cameron couldn't help but roll his eyes. "You're not seriously wearing that tonight, are you? You've got something else to change into, right?"

"What's wrong with this? The shorts and shirt are both new. See, no holes," Sam said as he spun in a circle to demonstrate.

"Just because it's new doesn't mean it's good," Cameron said, and Sam laughed.

"Then what, oh fashion guru, would you suggest?"

"You have some nice stuff you wear to work in the office, right? Grab one of those outfits. The gray slacks with that green, kind of satiny shirt look good on you." It looked more than good. Cameron had had to spend some quality time in his room the first time Sam came home wearing that outfit, and Cameron didn't even go for the "shirt and tie" thing, at least not before Sam.

"It's just going to be family and friends. I don't really think they expect me to dress up." Cameron simply stared at him with his eyebrows raised until Sam huffed out a breath and rolled his eyes. "Fine. But that shirt's at the cleaners."

"So pick it up on your way home this afternoon, and it'll be nice and clean and pressed—perfect for the party."

Cameron smiled sweetly at him, and Sam gave him a sour look in return, but Cameron was pretty sure he'd see the outfit in question that night. Now, if only getting Sam to put out was that easy.

"Come on, fashion guru. It's my birthday, so you need to let me kick your ass at something before I head out. You pick the game," Sam said as he made his way to the couch.

They'd spent the last twenty-four hours making Sam's house spotless for the party, so there really wasn't much else they could do without messing up all their hard work. Cameron plunked down on the couch and grabbed his controller while Sam did the same, and they killed a couple of hours, and a few more brain cells, getting sucked into the game.

The doorbell rang shortly before noon, and Sam paused the game and hopped off the couch to get it. Cameron set his controller down with a little less enthusiasm and stood, with butterflies in his stomach, as he heard voices call out "Happy birthday!" in unison and two men preceded Sam into the room. The first guy was as short as Cameron, with a soul patch on his chin, black curly hair, and glasses. Cameron would've said he wasn't bad-looking except for the "I just smelled something rotten" expression on his face as his eyes raked Cameron up and down. The other guy was taller, over six feet, and blond, with nice blue eyes and an open smile as he glanced expectantly between Cameron and Sam, waiting to be introduced.

"Cameron, this is Ryan and his partner John." Sam waved a hand at each man respectively. "Guys, this is Cameron. He has graciously offered to help you out with anything you need, while I make myself scarce during the party preparations. He knows where everything is, so just ask him if you can't find something."

"It's nice to finally meet you, Cameron," John said, extending his hand for a quick shake.

Ryan didn't make a move until John's elbow bumped his partner, as John withdrew from their handshake, and only then did the other man extend his own hand, with obvious reluctance. "It's nice to meet you," he said.

Cameron was pretty sure the guy didn't mean it, but he smiled anyway and said, "You too. Sam talks about you all the time. And, like he said, I'll help out any way you want me to."

Cameron felt his stomach twist a little as the two men shared a look. He had no idea what it meant, but he had a bad feeling Ryan wasn't going to get any friendlier, no matter how helpful Cameron tried to be.

"I guess that's my cue to hit the road," Sam said with a laugh as he clapped the two men on the shoulders. "The folding chairs and extra table we borrowed from the neighbor are on the back porch, and everything's as clean as we could make it."

Ryan smiled for the first time and kissed Sam on the cheek before making shooing motions at him. "Get out of here and don't come back until five at the earliest, okay?"

"Yeah, I got it. Play nice you guys," Sam said as he grabbed his keys and wallet off the breakfast bar and headed out the door, giving

Cameron an encouraging smile and a wave over his shoulder, before closing it behind him.

There was an awkward silence after Sam left, and Cameron shuffled his feet and chewed on his lip ring until John clapped his hands together and smiled. "Okay Cameron, we have a bunch of bags in the back of the car that need to come in, if you'd like to help us with that?"

"Sure. Just tell me where you want them." Cameron could feel Ryan's eyes on him as he followed John out, but he tried to ignore the man. He didn't know what Ryan's problem was, but John seemed nice enough, so maybe this afternoon wouldn't be a total nightmare.

As the day wore on, though, Ryan only got pissier and pissier. It didn't seem to matter how nice Cameron tried to be, or how helpful John said he was. When the two men finally left to go get the rest of the food and supplies, Cameron went back to his room and collapsed onto his bed with a sigh of relief. He'd been getting more and more anxious and irritable all afternoon, but he knew if he said anything to Ryan or to Sam about it, it would probably only make things worse, and maybe even ruin Sam's birthday, so he decided to keep his mouth shut and avoid Ryan as much as he could.

Cameron's decision was tested immediately upon their return, when Ryan refused to let him carry any of the wine or beer inside.

"You're underage," Ryan said with a smirk. "Sam would never forgive us if we made you carry the booze."

Cameron almost lost it when Ryan started making little passive-aggressive comments to John about what a pain in the ass it was that they had to make Kool-Aid or lemonade for the underage crowd as he walked past Cameron and into the house.

John might have seen something in Cameron's face, or maybe he knew what an asshole his boyfriend was, because he immediately spoke up, trying to smooth things over. "Sam's sister and niece prefer iced tea anyway, so it's no big deal."

Ryan didn't seem to have a snappy comeback for that one, so he sniffed and walked off to work on something in the backyard, and John gave Cameron an apologetic smile and went back to emptying the bags onto the breakfast bar.

"Is there anything else I can help you with?" Cameron said, leaning over the bar and looking up at John through his eyelashes.

"Uh, sure. Why don't you cut up the carrots and stuff for the veggie tray?" John tried to move out of the way as Cameron came into the kitchen, but Cameron brushed up against him as he passed anyway. John was blushing a little when Cameron smiled at him over his shoulder, and Cameron couldn't seem to stop himself from sashaying a little as he continued across the small space to bend over and pull the cutting board out.

Later, Cameron would blame his behavior on pent-up sexual frustration, several weeks in the making, and maybe wanting to get back at Ryan for being such a dick. But at that moment, he wasn't really thinking about what he was doing. He was simply reacting in a way that came all too naturally for him. John's shy responsiveness to his flirting was like chumming the water, and Cameron's ego was definitely in need of some stroking.

"John?" he called out sweetly to the other man, who'd gone into the living room to work on the decorations.

"Yeah?"

"Would you come here and help me with something?" When John came back into the kitchen, Cameron walked over close to him and pointed to the stack of plates on top of the cabinets, above the refrigerator. "Do you think you can reach up there for one of the platters? I'd go get a chair, but I figure it would be easier to ask someone tall."

John's grin was a little goofy as he reached for the platters in question, and Cameron purposefully let his eyes drift down the man's torso as he stretched to get it, only swinging his eyes back up when he was sure he'd been caught looking. "Thanks," Cameron said and bit his lip a little as John handed the plate over.

John cleared his throat. "Sure, no problem."

The poor guy hurried outside to help his boyfriend after that, so Cameron figured that was his cue to lay off. He wasn't seriously trying to bag the guy, but it was hard to hold back when John responded to him so nicely.

Thankfully, John stayed close to his boyfriend, and Ryan stayed far away from Cameron, only speaking to him when absolutely necessary, over the next few hours, as Sam's house was transformed into party central. And despite Ryan's attitude, it was kind of fun for Cameron to be involved in the behind-the-scenes of a real, grown-up party for once.

He was used to impromptu house parties where people showed up with bags of junk food, booze, and drugs, and everyone plopped down on any available surface and got wasted while music pounded around them. And the parties at Sean's had always been catered, with Sean hiring some guy to organize it all and then wandering off to get high or get laid until his guests started arriving, so all this setup and planning was a new and interesting experience for Cameron.

By the time they finished with Sam's house, Cameron was actually excited to see how all their efforts would pay off. Ryan hadn't really let him do much, but what furniture he had moved or what platters he'd been allowed to fill were still an accomplishment, and he was feeling pretty proud when Sam came in the door at five.

The smile on Sam's face was worth every minute Cameron had held his tongue that afternoon, especially when Sam pulled him in for a quick hug in thanks for helping out. The hug was way too brief, and only around the shoulders, but it was better than nothing. Sam smelled like the beach and sunshine and clean sweat, and Cameron was pretty sure the memory of it would feature in his fantasies for a while.

"Oh my God. The place looks great! Thank you guys for this," Sam said as he draped the bag from the cleaners over a chair and took a look around.

"Happy birthday, Sam," Ryan said, his voice gentler than Cameron had heard it all day. The tenderness in the smile Ryan gave to Sam almost made Cameron forget what a prick the guy was for a second, until Ryan caught him watching, and the smile dropped away like it had never been.

"I'm going to hit the shower and get changed, unless you guys need my help with anything," Sam said, breaking in on the tableau between the two of them.

Ryan shook his head. "You go ahead. We're pretty much done here." He and John walked toward the kitchen while Sam headed to the bathroom, and Cameron frowned after the couple. He still had no idea what the fuck Ryan's problem was.

When Sam came back into the living room a short while later, Cameron was sitting on the couch by himself, while Ryan and John appeared to be having a serious conversation in the backyard. They'd flipped the couch around and moved it in front of the TV for the party, so it gave Cameron perfect front-row seats to the fight between the lovers. Cameron supposed he could have gone back to his room to give them some privacy, but part of him was kind of enjoying watching John tell his boyfriend off, even if he couldn't actually hear what was being said.

Of course, when Sam came into the room, dressed in Cameron's favorite outfit, he forgot all about the two in the yard and simply stared at the man. Sam looked good, *really* good. He wasn't wearing a tie, like he usually did when he wore that shirt for work, and he'd left the top couple of buttons open at his neck and rolled up the sleeves, but that only served to draw attention to the man's chest and nicely muscled forearms. Cameron stifled a whimper of frustrated lust and kept his mouth clamped shut so he wouldn't say anything stupid.

"Hey," Sam said when he spotted Cameron on the couch. "Is this acceptable, oh fashion guru, or do I need to put on the tie too?"

Cameron forced a laugh. "It's acceptable. You want something to drink?" Cameron hopped up from the couch and headed to kitchen before any of his thoughts could be read on his face. He grabbed a beer out of one of the coolers on the floor by the door to the laundry room and cracked it open without thinking. He'd barely put it to his lips when the bottle was taken from his hands.

"Sorry kid, not gonna happen," Sam said, before putting the bottle to his own lips and drinking.

Cameron's emotions vacillated between irritation at the "kid" comment and having his beer taken away and lust at watching Sam suck on the bottle he'd just had his mouth on. "You do realize I've done a hell of a lot more than drink a few beers in my life, right?"

Sam shrugged. "Still not gonna happen here, until you're twenty-one. Besides, after your night out a few weeks ago, I'd figured you wouldn't want anything to do with the stuff for a good long time to come."

Cameron rolled his eyes, but Sam had already turned around and headed back to the living room, so the gesture was wasted on him.

"What are those two arguing about?" Sam said as he stood in front of the sliding glass doors and watched the men in his backyard.

"I don't know. They didn't include me in their discussion."

Something in Cameron's tone made Sam turn around and look at him. "Is something wrong? Ryan didn't say anything to upset you, did he?"

Cameron really wanted to say "yes." He wanted to unload on Sam and tell him what a jerk his friend was and how mean he'd been all day, but he didn't. It was Sam's birthday, and if Cameron was going to show Sam what a nice *adult* he could be, bitching about his friend, right before his birthday party, would be a bad idea. Today wasn't supposed to be about Cameron. It was supposed to be about Sam. And even though it went completely contrary to Cameron's nature not to be self-absorbed, he figured he could manage it this one time.

"No. It was fine. No worries." Cameron gave him a sweet smile, but Sam didn't appear to be buying it. Fortunately, he was literally saved by the bell when Elena, Shawna, and Michael arrived.

Elena dragged in a giant "Happy 30th" balloon and a gift bag bursting with ribbons and tissue, while Michael brought up the rear with a box Cameron assumed contained Sam's birthday cake. "Happy birthday, baby brother!" she said as she handed over the balloon and bag and gave them both big hugs. Shawna and Michael came in behind her, and there were more greetings and more hugging, although Michael skipped hugging Cameron, and Cameron was fine with that.

When they all made their way into the living room, Ryan and John were already inside, all smiles, with no hint they'd been fighting nonstop for the last twenty minutes or so, and everyone sat down to chat until the rest of the guests started arriving.

Over the next couple of hours, a steady stream of people came through the front door, and Sam made the rounds, laughing and smiling. Despite all the people clamoring for his attention, Sam took time to introduce Cameron to most of his friends, but Cameron didn't really remember their names afterward, especially since most of them stopped talking to him the second Sam wandered away to greet other guests.

Cameron's hopes of making some new friends were quickly dashed as it became clear that Elena and Shawna were the only ones who seemed willing to hang out with him. All night Cameron felt eyes on him from different parts of the room, but whenever he made an effort to join in on the conversations around him, they died awkwardly shortly after he showed up. He tried not to let the stares bother him as he sat with Sam's family, but it wasn't easy, especially since he knew from some of the looks he was getting, if the hypocrites pretending to ignore him didn't have their boyfriends standing next to them, they'd probably be trying to get into his pants. But Sam seemed to be having such a great time that Cameron forced himself to take it and kept being good, up until Stefano arrived.

Stefano was a bronze god of a man. Tall, dark, and handsome were the first words that came to mind, even though they really didn't do him justice. He showed up four hours after the party started. They'd already done the cake and presents portion of the evening, and Elena and her family had already gone home because Michael wasn't feeling very well. So that left Cameron alone, without anyone to distract him, when Ryan brought the slick Italian into the room and made a beeline for Sam. Cameron was a little ways away from them, but even he heard when Ryan made a point of mentioning Stefano was new to the area and *single*. And Cameron was pretty sure he saw the asshole glance in his direction when he said it.

Cameron might have held it together even then, if he hadn't seen the obvious interest in the Italian's eyes as he gave Sam a once over, and even worse, the interest in Sam's eyes as he returned the look. But it took less than five minutes of watching the two men smile and flirt with each other for Cameron to see red.

It was bad enough he'd had to put up with Ryan's shit all day. Then he had to hang out at a party where everyone treated him like shit, while staring at him behind his back. But now, he had to watch the man he was falling hard for flirt with some hot guy Ryan had obviously invited as a setup, and there wasn't anything he could do about it.

Cameron clenched his teeth against the sea of emotion threatening to drown him and made a break for his room. Thankfully, there wasn't anyone in the back of the house, except someone using the bathroom, so his bedroom was empty when he got there. Cameron rushed inside, closed his door, and leaned his back against it, simply breathing with his eyes closed for several moments. He could feel the tension, anxiety, and unhappiness swelling inside him, and he wasn't sure he could handle it without doing something stupid. The only thing that stopped him from bursting into tears or throwing something at Ryan, or Stefano, or Sam—or all three of them for that matter—was the fear of doing something so incredibly embarrassing and obviously immature in front of all those people, people who already acted like he was some freak show attraction.

When he thought he could open his eyes without crying like a baby, Cameron stepped away from the door and went straight to the closet in the corner of his room. He dug through the pile of stuff in the bottom until he found his duffel bag and pulled out the pack of cigarettes he'd found in his jacket, after the night he'd gone out with his friends. He grabbed the lighter he kept for the candles Sam had bought him and was about to light up, when it occurred to him he really didn't want his room to smell like smoke any more than Sam did. Even cloves could make a room rank after a while.

He slunk back out into the hall and through the front door, without anyone really paying him any attention. He didn't even glance toward the living room, afraid of what he'd see if he did. As he walked around the side of the house and into the carport, Cameron made a detour through the side door into the laundry room. He snuck through to the kitchen, reached down into one of the coolers, and grabbed a couple of beers for himself before going back out the way he'd come.

It was after eleven and the sun had gone down a couple of hours ago, so Cameron found himself a dark little corner in the backyard, away from everyone else, and sat down in the thick grass. He lit up a cigarette and opened his beer, raising it in mock salute to all the happy partygoers before downing half of it in one long swallow. He let out a satisfied burp, leaned back against the rough wood fence, and stared up at the stars while he puffed away at his cancer stick and polished off the first beer before moving on to the second.

He'd finished his second beer and third cigarette and was contemplating whether to light up a fourth or make another foray to the kitchen when a shadow fell over him, blocking the lights from the back of the house.

"Is this seat taken?" John asked.

Cameron smiled—*finally*, a friendly face. "Nope."

John sat down on the ground next to him and leaned back against the fence with a sigh. "Can I bum one of those?" he asked pointing at the pack of cigarettes on Cameron's thigh.

Cameron pulled out another for himself and handed the pack and lighter to John. John lit up and took a few puffs before groaning in pleasure. "Do you know how long it's been since I had one of these?"

Cameron shook his head and put his own cigarette to his lips, and John lit it for him.

"Too long," John answered. "I know they're bad for me, and I know they smell terrible on your clothes and your hair and your breath, but *Gawd*, sometimes I could kill for a good smoke."

Cameron couldn't help but chuckle. Maybe it was the beer, he didn't know, but he felt himself relaxing as John's deep voice rolled over him.

They were silent for a little while longer before John spoke again. "Ryan is going to kill me when he smells it on me, but right now, I don't really care." John paused there for a few moments, and Cameron could feel the other man looking at him. "I'm sorry he was so shitty to you today. You really were a big help. I know he loves Sam a lot and he's really protective of anyone he cares about, but he shouldn't have treated you like that."

Cameron smiled and fluttered his eyelashes at the man. "I know how you can make it up to me. Get me a refill or two?" he said, waving his empty beer bottle.

John looked at him for a second, pursing his lips like he was going to say no, but then he glanced down at the two empty beer bottles Cameron already had and shrugged. "Yeah, okay. I could use another too. I'm not sure I can make it through the house without being spotted and waylaid, but I'll try."

"Take the secret entrance through the carport. That's what I did."

John grinned at him a little too broadly and got unsteadily to his feet. "Be right back."

Cameron had a feeling John didn't really need any more beer either, but the guy was good to look at, and the only one there being nice to him, so he wasn't going to be the one preaching moderation.

"There were only three left in the cooler by the door, so I snagged them," John said as he plunked back down beside him and handed over a bottle.

"Thanks."

John was sitting closer this time, but Cam didn't mind. He hadn't brought his jacket out, and the extra warmth felt kind of nice as the night air cooled around them.

"So I never did get the full story on how you ended up with Sam," John said after downing half his beer.

Cameron glanced over at him, wondering if maybe John was trying to be the good cop to Ryan's bad cop, pumping him for information, but the other man was only looking at him with an innocent, somewhat glazed expression, so he figured why the hell not?

"Sam's sister was my English teacher. I got kicked out of my mom and stepdad's and was staying with someone else for a while, but that got pretty fucked-up. So I called Elena, and she said I could stay with her. But her husband flipped, and when Shawna came home, he said I had to find someplace else, and Sam was nice enough to let me stay here until I can get my shit together."

"Sam's a really nice guy," John said slowly.

"Yeah, he is." Cameron felt something painful twist in his chest, and he took a swig of his beer before lighting up another cigarette.

"I'm sorry about your family. That must've been really hard," John said, before he took the cigarette out of Cam's fingers and took a drag from it.

"Yeah."

John offered the cigarette back, and Cameron took it. He didn't have much to add that wouldn't have him in tears, so he kept his mouth shut. He was feeling lonely and unwanted. And Sam was in the house being pawed by some hot stranger, probably letting the guy give him the kind of birthday present he'd never let Cameron give him.

Some of what he was feeling must have shown on his face, because even in the dark, John picked up on it, despite the fact he attributed it to the wrong thing. "Oh sweetie, I'm so sorry. Nobody in the world can hurt us quite like our parents."

John scooted closer and wrapped his arms around Cameron. It was awkward at first, given they were sitting on the ground next to each other, but Cameron twisted into the hug, burying his face in John's neck and closing his eyes. John petted his hair and stroked his back for a long time, until Cameron started to feel warm all over. John probably would have left it at that, if Cameron hadn't made the next move. But Cam was feeling neglected, pissed off, and insecure. Add in a bit of alcohol, and that was *always* a recipe for him to do something stupid.

He started by nibbling on John's neck. The other man jumped a little in surprise but didn't pull away, and when John moaned, Cameron felt a surge of heat shoot straight to his groin, short-circuiting any attempts his brain might have made at reason. Cameron pulled back only enough to grab John's face and bring the man's mouth down for a kiss, and kiss they did. It was warm, and wet, and sexy, and Cameron didn't really give a shit who it was he was kissing… at least not until "What the fuck!" was screeched at them from across the yard.

John launched himself away from Cameron, ending up flat on his back in the dirt, before he scrambled clumsily to his feet, facing his raging boyfriend.

"You fucking little bitch!" Ryan launched himself at Cameron, and Cameron was lucky John was there to stop the man, or he might have gotten his ass kicked before he could even clear his head enough to know what hit him.

"Get off me, you asshole!" Ryan screeched again as he shoved his boyfriend.

By this time, Cameron had scrambled to his feet, and all eyes at the party were on their little scene. When he saw Sam and Stefano come out the sliding glass doors and head toward them, Cameron groaned and wished he could find a rock to crawl under.

"What's going on?" Sam asked, as soon as he was close enough.

"Ask your pet slut," Ryan yelled as John continued to plead with him.

Sam's eyes turned to him in confusion, taking in the empty beer bottles and cigarette butts on the ground. Cameron opened his mouth to explain, but nothing came out. He looked back and forth between Sam and Ryan, feeling Stefano's curious gaze on him the whole time, and all he could manage was a barely audible "I'm sorry, Sam."

When disappointment and suspicion started to replace the confusion in Sam's eyes, Cameron felt the first sign of tears prickling his own, and he fought them down with all he had.

"Fine!" Ryan shouted, drawing everyone's eyes back to him. "I'm gone! But you tell that little shit if he even looks at you again, I'll kick his ass!" Ryan stormed off toward the house with John on his heels, and after one last glance at Cameron, Sam and the rest of the guests followed them back into the house, leaving Cameron alone.

He dropped back down onto the ground and pulled his knees to his chest, wrapping his arms around them and hugging himself tight. He felt dizzy and sick, and he couldn't blame all of that on the beer and cigarettes. He'd fucked up, *again*.

Why? Why did he always do this shit? What the hell was wrong with him?

# CHAPTER ELEVEN

THE PARTY guests trickled out after that, leaving a heavy silence behind them. Ryan and John had originally volunteered to help clean up after the party, but that was before the scene in the yard. Now Sam was stuck with a house full of trash, food, decorations, and a drunken Cameron in his backyard.

*Happy birthday to me.*

Sam sighed and dragged a hand through his hair. Things had been going wonderfully up until the fight. He'd been having a blast catching up with all of his friends again and being flirted with by a seriously hot Italian man. Now he felt bad that he hadn't gotten the guy's number before he ran away with all the other guests, but since Ryan had been the one who invited him, Sam was pretty sure he could get Stefano's number, once Ryan cooled off enough to speak to him again.

Sam massaged his forehead, trying the ease the headache that had already started. First, he had to go deal with Cameron. Then he'd decide if he had the energy to mess with any of the cleanup, or if he'd just say, "fuck it," and leave it until the morning.

He found Cameron curled up on the ground, not far from where he'd left him. Sam stood over him for a while, trying to come up with something to say. When Cameron lifted his head and looked at Sam with those goddamned beautiful puppy dog eyes, Sam had to literally stiffen his spine. He needed to stay mad, and it wasn't something that came naturally to him. "Jesus, Cameron. I don't even…." He stopped, unsure of what he was trying to say.

Cameron chewed on his lip and looked toward the house. "Is everybody gone?"

"Yeah."

The kid blew out a breath and struggled to his feet. "I'm sorry."

"You've said that before. Why, Cameron? Why would you do such a thing?"

As Sam waited, Cameron fidgeted for a few moments before he lowered his head and shrugged. "I didn't mean to do it. I was feeling shitty, and he was being nice to me, hugging me, and it just kind of happened."

"Are you saying John took advantage of you?"

Cameron's head came up quickly. "No! No. It's my fault… like always. I came out here to be alone, and he came out to talk, that's all. I think he felt sorry for me."

"Why would he feel sorry for you?"

Cameron shrugged again, and when it looked like that was the only response Sam was going to get, he said, "Not good enough, Cameron. Talk to me."

Cameron chewed on his lip and shifted from foot to foot some more. "No one wanted to talk to me. They all stared at me behind my back, but they ignored me when I tried to be nice. And after this afternoon, I was already on edge, so I took a couple of beers and went out for a smoke or two, to calm down. That's all."

"You know I didn't want you drinking in my house."

The corner of Cameron's mouth lifted in a half smile. "I wasn't actually in your house when I did it." Sam glared at him, and Cameron ducked his head again. "Sorry."

"Let's get back to the other thing. Why were you on edge from this afternoon?"

Cameron looked away from him. "I lied earlier, when you asked if Ryan said anything to me."

"Shit. What did he say?"

He looked back at Sam. "It wasn't so much what he said as how he treated me, how he talked to me. He wasn't very nice. And I tried to be nice, Sam. I tried to ignore him. I swear."

"So that led to you making out with his boyfriend tonight?"

"I didn't plan it. He came out and started talking to me, and it just happened."

Sam groaned and dropped his face into his hands for a few moments before blowing out a breath and raising his head again. "Come on. Let's go inside." He felt Cameron follow as he led the way back up to the deck and into the living room. His house was just as much of a mess as it had been a few minutes ago, but Sam tried to ignore it as he dropped down onto the couch and motioned for Cameron to do the same. Sam leaned back against the cushions, draped an arm over his eyes, and tried to think through his rapidly receding buzz and sudden exhaustion.

When he opened his eyes, he found Cameron still watching him anxiously, and he sighed. "Look. I'm sorry Ryan wasn't nice to you. He promised to behave, and I took him at his word. But he's terrible at hiding his feelings, and I should have remembered that. I should have stayed until I was sure you guys were getting along. I guess I assumed John would keep the peace, like he always does." Sam let out a snort. "I guess I was wrong."

Cameron's eyes were suspiciously bright as he stared at Sam and shook his head. "It's not your fault. I fucked up, Sam. I wanted this birthday to be so great for you, and I still managed to fuck it up."

Sam's heart melted a little, and he reached out to put a hand over the fists Cameron had clenched in his lap. "It wasn't all fucked up, Cameron. I had a great time, up until the grand finale anyway. On the plus side, it was a party that won't be easily forgotten."

Cameron gave him a watery smile, and Sam gave him a tired chuckle in return. "Don't worry about it. We're going to fix this. Not tonight, because I'm still working off my buzz, and I'm way too tired to think straight, but tomorrow. Tomorrow, we're going to talk to them and fix this, provided Ryan has calmed down enough to actually take my call. Okay?"

"Yeah, okay," Cameron said quietly.

Sam patted Cameron's hands before pulling back and climbing to his feet. "I think I've had enough fun for today. I'm going to bed. We'll worry about all this in the morning," he said as he walked past all the decorations, food, and drinks strewn all over his living room. "Lock up for me, will you?"

Sam didn't turn around to see if Cameron responded. He was completely worn out, and all he wanted was to crash. Tomorrow was another day, and he'd figure everything out after he'd had a good night's sleep.

THE SUN was way too bright as it filtered through his blinds the next morning. Luckily for Sam, Cesar had insisted he not come into the shop the whole weekend, saying it was his chance to prove to the boss-man he could handle the place all on his own. Sam looked at the clock by his bed and groaned. He'd slept in to nearly ten o'clock, and he still felt like he'd been hit by a bus. Maybe he'd had more to drink than he thought.

As he slid his legs over the side of the bed and sat up, Sam remembered the mess waiting for him outside his bedroom, and he groaned again, cradling his head in his hands. He didn't even want to think about it, but the mess wasn't going to disappear by him sitting in bed, so he climbed slowly to his feet and shuffled into the hallway.

The first thing that hit him as he came into the living room was the heavenly smell of fresh-brewed coffee. The second was a little harder for his sleepy brain to grasp, but when it did, Sam actually thought he heard angels singing. The living room was completely clean, not a single plate or decoration to be found, and all the furniture was back where it belonged. A quick glance outside and into the dining room, on his way to the kitchen, showed him they'd been cleaned up as well. The kitchen had stacks of plastic containers and Ziploc bags on one counter, but the rest of the room was spotless, and the coffee pot was warm and waiting for him.

As Sam sat at the breakfast bar, sipping his coffee and looking around him in happy surprise, Cameron came in through the door to the laundry room. His hair was a wild mess of curls, he had his glasses on, and he was wearing one of Sam's old grubby T-shirts. Sam thought he'd never looked better.

"Hey," Sam said.

Cameron started and glanced up at him warily. "Hey."

Sam softened his expression and gave Cameron his most grateful smile. "Thank you for cleaning up. You didn't have to do that all on your own."

Cameron shrugged. "It's kind of my fault your helpers left."

Sam couldn't deny his logic, but he was still touched Cameron had volunteered to do it, especially when he spotted the dark circles under the man's eyes. "Did you sleep at all?"

"Yeah, a little."

As Cameron stood there, looking exhausted and guilty, Sam couldn't take it anymore. He stood up and pulled him into a hug. "It's okay, Cameron. Everything's going to be okay."

Cameron was stiff in his arms, so Sam let go pretty quickly and put some space between them, smiling to ease the awkwardness of the moment. Perhaps it was still too soon for him to be his touchy-feely self.

"Do you want some breakfast?" Cameron asked, breaking the silence that followed.

"You cooking?" Sam laughed, hoping to put them back on familiar ground, and it worked. Cameron smiled.

"Yeah."

He made eggs, sausage, and toast, while Sam lounged out back and drank his coffee. There were definite benefits to having Cameron feel guilty, although Sam would rather not have a repeat of the events leading up to it. When Cameron brought the plate out to him a little while later, he set a thin brown paper shopping bag down next to it on the table.

"What's this?"

Cameron shrugged. "Your birthday present. I was going to give it to you yesterday, but I felt kind of stupid having you open it in front of all your other friends, especially after I saw all the other gifts they brought you. But I got it for you, so I figured you might as well have it, even if it's nothing special."

It bothered him a lot that Cameron was too embarrassed to give him his gift in front of his friends, but he didn't say anything about it because he wasn't sure how to fix it. He opened the bag and pulled out the somewhat tattered paperback inside: *Classic Rock: 50 Favorites for Easy Guitar*.

"I know it's not much," Cameron said, "but I found it at the used book store near the library, and I thought you'd like it."

Sam was really tempted to get up and give Cameron another hug, but he restrained himself. "Thank you, Cameron. This is great. Looks like I'll have plenty of time to mess around with it, since you've already cleaned up."

Cameron's smile wasn't hesitant or guilty this time. It was bright and happy, and it lightened Sam's heart to see it. "And we have enough food for a week, so neither one of us has to cook dinner either," Cameron said with a laugh.

Sam hated to ruin the mood by reminding him of the loose ends they still had to tie up with Ryan and John, so he decided to take a couple of hours to play around with his guitar and show Cameron how much he appreciated his gift. They had breakfast and took turns plucking out notes from the book until Cameron started yawning and eventually had to excuse himself for a nap. After he left, Sam decided to make the first attempt at smoothing things over with Ryan. He wasn't very optimistic, but he called Ryan's cell first and then John's.

They both went straight to voice mail, and he left messages for each of them, but it wasn't until almost dinnertime that Ryan finally called him back.

"Hey." Ryan's voice was scratchy, and he sounded exhausted.

"Hey there. I'd ask if everything was okay, but since you sound like shit, I'm going to assume that would be a no."

Ryan chuckled, surprising him. "You might say that. But, actually, I think everything is going to be fine. We stayed up pretty late talking last night, something we haven't done in a long time, and after we both sobered up, the talking was actually constructive."

"Oh good."

Ryan laughed again. "Yeah. You might say I was a *little* angry at first, but eventually we worked on some things we'd both been ignoring for way too long. I might even call it a blessing in disguise, if I weren't still pretty pissed off at that little—"

"Ryan," Sam said sharply, cutting his friend off before he could get started.

"I have a right to be pissed at him, Sam… and worried about you for taking him in."

"Don't start. Yes, you have a right to be pissed off about what he did. He's sorry, and he wants to apologize to both of you, if you'll let him."

Ryan growled on the other end of the line, and Sam sighed loudly enough for his friend to hear his irritation. "Look. I appreciate that you're worried about me, really. But I'm a big boy, and I know Cameron a lot better than you do. You're going to have to trust me when I tell you he's a good person who's been through a lot of shit, and he's just a little messed up right now. He's willing to try, Ryan, and I'd appreciate it if you'd give him a chance, for me."

When Ryan continued to be silent, Sam huffed. "Look. I know he messed up, but you weren't exactly an angel either. You promised me you'd be nice to him, and you weren't even close."

"Is that what he told you? That I was mean to him?"

"Weren't you?"

Silence again, and then Ryan grumbled, "Okay, *fine*. I may have been a little unfriendly. But that isn't an excuse for what he did."

"I agree, and that's why he wants to apologize. It would be nice if maybe you took the opportunity to apologize to him as well."

"Don't push your luck, Sam."

Sam smiled and shook his head, even though Ryan couldn't see him do it. "It was just a thought. Look, how about we do dinner sometime soon, the four of us?"

Ryan sighed. "Yeah. We need to come over there anyway, to help you clean and to pick up our stuff. You want us to come over now?"

"Only if you want to," Sam replied. "Cameron already cleaned everything up, so you don't have to worry about that. There is a ton of food still here, if you'd like to help us eat some of it, though. I even have some birthday cake left."

"The kid cleaned up? By himself?"

Sam rolled his eyes. "Like I told you already, you don't know him, Ryan. He's a good person."

"So you say."

Instead of biting his head off, like he really wanted to, Sam decided to go a different route. "You know," he said, conversationally, "there have been a lot of people over the years who've disagreed with me when I've tried to convince them you were a good person underneath all the asshole."

"Touché," Ryan said with a laugh. "Okay. Let me talk to John. If he's okay with it, we'll be by in an hour or so. Is that fine with you?"

"That will do nicely," Sam replied primly.

They said their good-byes, and Sam climbed out of his chair on the deck, stopping when he found Cameron waiting for him at the door, looking nervous. Sam wasn't sure how much he'd heard, so he said, "That was Ryan. He and John will be over in a little while to pick up their stuff and help us eat some of that food. Are you still good with sitting down with them and repairing the damage?"

Cameron swallowed and nodded hesitantly, and Sam chuckled and shook the kid's shoulder a little as he passed by him. "Don't worry. Ryan doesn't bite. He barks a lot, and he's still pissed, but he can act like a grown-up when he has to."

Sam was pleased to see Cameron seemed a little comforted by his words. "Okay. I'm going to go take a shower and get changed."

Sam actually opened his mouth to tell Cameron not to bother, to say he kind of liked the dirty look on him, but he changed his mind pretty quickly. He didn't figure the joke would go over very well, especially since he meant it. Instead, he clamped his mouth shut again and made exaggerated shooing motions to cover his discomfort, and Cameron turned and headed off to the bathroom after giving him a bemused smile.

When he was gone, Sam shook off the weirdness of the moment and went back to his room to change out of his sleep shorts and T-shirt and into a pair of cargo shorts and another T-shirt. When he glanced at his reflection in the mirror, he laughed at himself, thinking it was hardly worth the effort to change, but it was a matter of principle, he supposed. He wouldn't spend the entire day in his pajamas, even if it was his Sunday off.

When John and Ryan showed up a little while later, Cameron and Sam had already set up the table on the porch with place settings for four and filled some platters with bits and pieces of the leftovers from the party. Sam purposefully filled two pitchers for the table, one with iced tea and one with water and lemon, because he didn't want anyone drinking tonight. He wanted everyone sober and on an equal footing.

Things were a little tense to start out. Both John and Cameron were watching Ryan warily, as if he might explode any second, and Sam was watching all three of them in exasperation. When it became obvious Ryan was going to behave himself, they all seemed to relax a little, and Sam made sure to keep the conversation light while they ate. Mostly they talked about the guests who'd showed up for the party, although Sam felt a little bad that Cameron didn't have much to add to the conversation. But a few glances in his direction told him that the kid actually seemed to be enjoying listening to the stories, even if he didn't know the people involved, so he didn't bother changing the subject.

When the food was gone and silence descended on the group, Sam decided they'd danced around the subject long enough and said, "So who's going to go first?"

All three of his table companions looked at him like deer stuck in the headlights, until Cameron cleared his throat and croaked, "I guess that would be me?"

He said it as a question, but Sam figured, by the death grip the kid had on his water glass, he already knew the answer. "Go ahead, Cameron."

"I'm sorry. Both of you. I… got a little drunk, and I did something really stupid and hurtful. I promise it won't ever happen again."

"Damn right it won't," Ryan said under his breath. Sam frowned at his friend, and John swatted his partner's shoulder. "Ouch. What?"

"What do you mean, 'what'?" John fumed. "We talked about this last night. Quit acting like a shit. He wasn't the only one involved, Ryan, and we've both apologized to you for screwing up. You can't accept my apology and ignore his."

Ryan glanced around the table and then threw up his hands. "Fine. I accept your apology."

"And?" John said, staring at his partner expectantly.

Ryan huffed and looked out across the yard sourly. "And I'm sorry if I was a dick yesterday."

The words were stilted, like he was reading them from a script, but Sam guessed that was the best they were going to get out of him, less than twenty-four hours after Cameron had made out with his partner, so he didn't push for more.

"Great," Sam said into the strained silence that followed. "Now my friends can all get along well enough around each other that I don't have to worry about fist fights breaking out. Thank you." His sardonic tone wasn't missed by anyone at the table. John rolled his eyes, but he smiled. Ryan's lips twisted into the semblance of a smile, and Cameron snorted quietly as he looked at Sam with gratitude and relief shining in his eyes. "Anyone for cake?"

# CHAPTER TWELVE

THE NEXT few weeks before he took his GED passed quickly for Cameron. He and Sam fell back into their old routine with only one unfortunate exception. After the party, Sam started going out a lot more than he had before, as old friends he'd reconnected with called him up to invite him to dinner or to the parties they were throwing. Sam said it was because they finally had proof he'd emerged from his hibernation after his ex had moved out, and Cameron laughed and pretended not to be too hurt that he wasn't invited to any of these events. After all, they were *Sam's* friends, not his, right? Cameron wasn't his boyfriend, so Sam wasn't obligated to invite him along. At least, that's what he tried to tell himself.

On the nights Sam wasn't there, Cameron filled his hours with studying and his fruitless efforts to find a job that wouldn't make him miserable. And when Sam *was* there, Cameron tried really hard to remind himself being Sam's friend was better than not having him in his life at all. Luckily, if Sam ever hooked up with that Stefano guy again, he never mentioned it, so Cameron didn't have to have that image burned into his brain. He could at least pretend Sam wasn't dating or fucking anyone when he was gone until late into the night.

The day of the big test, Sam took off work to drive him there and lend him moral support like the wonderful man he was. When they arrived, Cameron felt like he was going to lose his shit before he even made it into the building, but Sam must have picked up on that pretty quick, because he actually got out of the car and wrapped his arms around him, hugging him for the first time since the party.

"You're going to do great. You got this," Sam whispered to him and then gave him a firm shove toward the doors.

Cameron appreciated the thought, and really appreciated the hug, but if Sam wanted him to calm down, that wasn't exactly the way to do it. At least the physical contact and warm breath against his ear and neck directed blood flow away from his currently freaking out brain enough to get him in the building without breaking down. But it wasn't until the doors were closed and the test placed in front of him that he was able to focus on the reason he was there.

Seven torturous hours later, Cameron wandered out into the parking lot and dropped down into the passenger seat of Sam's old clunker, feeling drained of any possibility of coherent thought.

"You okay?" Sam asked with a chuckle, although Cameron could see the concern in his eyes.

"Yeah. I think so." It was an effort, but Cameron dredged up a smile. "No. Brain. Left."

Sam laughed loudly, and his eyes were smiling as he said, "Come on, let's go get some food to celebrate. I'm sure you're starving."

As they sat across from each other in a booth at some diner Cameron had never been to before, Sam sipped on his milkshake while Cameron inhaled a burger and fries.

"I'm proud of you, Cameron. You did it," Sam finally said when Cameron stopped stuffing his face long enough to breathe.

He shrugged. "You don't know if I passed yet."

"You passed. I know you did. All we have to do is wait for the paper that confirms it."

Cameron stifled the smitten, teenaged-girl sigh threatening to escape as he looked up into Sam's smiling face, and he rolled his eyes instead. "Yeah, okay. We'll see."

"Yeah, we will," Sam said as he snagged one of the few remaining fries from Cameron's plate.

That night, they hung out together like normal. They messed around with Sam's dad's guitar and then played a little *Guitar Hero*, so Cameron could get some of his own back after his pathetic performance on the real thing. They had a great time like they always did when it was just the two of them. Cameron almost didn't mind that they went to separate beds at the end of it. He still had to spend some time with his right hand before he could sleep, but eventually he nodded off with a sense of relief that he'd completed the first step toward his future.

THE NEXT six weeks were a little anticlimactic. All of the sudden, he didn't have anything to fill his days anymore. He'd learned pretty quickly he wasn't going to be able to get even a semidecent retail job without his certificate in his hand. There were too many college kids out of school for the summer looking for work. And he couldn't even think about taking classes at the community college until he had his results, so he was kind of stuck in a holding pattern.

To help make up for the fact that he was still mooching off of Sam, Cameron took on all the household chores and cooked all the meals they ate together. He even did a bit of the yard work, though the lawn mower kind of scared the shit out of him, and he didn't exactly know what he was doing. Sam always said it was the thought that counted, but Cameron could tell the guy was laughing at him on the inside. Cameron didn't mind. Like he'd said before, Sam was pretty damned hot when he laughed.

Though he was a little ashamed to admit it, Cameron did break down and go out partying with his friends a few more times during those weeks. It was always on the nights when he knew Sam was out with his own friends, and Cameron was alone at the house, bouncing off the walls, imagining Sam hooking up with someone. He managed not to get completely wasted on those few occasions, and he only swapped a couple of blowjobs with random guys to take the edge off. He didn't fuck any of them, but he still felt guilty about it afterward, like he'd somehow failed himself.

The day his certificate and official test scores finally arrived, Cameron was bouncing off the walls for a different reason. He'd already checked some of his scores online, so he knew he'd passed, but he hadn't shared any of that with Sam yet, and he could hardly wait for Sam to get home from work so he could show him the envelope.

When he heard Sam's car pull up, Cameron stopped what he was doing in the kitchen, grabbed the envelope off the breakfast bar, and rushed to the door, practically vibrating with excitement. Sam was on the phone when he came in, so Cameron waited impatiently—with the envelope behind his back—for him to finish.

"You lied. This isn't a much-needed vacation. This is a setup," Sam said into his phone as he smiled at Cameron in greeting. "You know, I am capable of getting my own dates." He paused and Cameron could hear someone talking, although he couldn't quite make out what the person was saying. "A long weekend, out in the middle of nowhere, seems a bit extreme. What if we end up hating each other?" The voice talked again, and Sam laughed throatily as the happy smile fell from Cameron's face. "Yeah, yeah. He was pretty hot. Okay Ryan, look, I'm home now, and I'm starving, so let me think about it, and I'll call you back in a little while, okay?" Sam ended the call and gave Cameron another of his beautiful smiles. "Hey. Something smells great."

"Thanks," Cameron replied, with far less enthusiasm than he would have only a few minutes before. "I made empanadas from scratch, stuffed jalapenos, and I tried a flan recipe. I don't make any guarantees, but I think they turned out all right."

"That's fantastic," Sam said as he followed Cameron to the kitchen and set his keys, phone, and wallet on the breakfast bar. "What's that?" he asked, pointing to the envelope Cameron tossed on top of the microwave.

Cameron shrugged. "My test results came."

"Oh my God, that's great!" His eyes searched Cameron's face. "You don't seem too happy about it. Is everything okay?"

Cameron shrugged again and handed the envelope over to him. Sam threw him one last concerned look before opening the envelope and scanning the papers inside. "Jesus, Cameron! You had me worried. These are fantastic scores. Why aren't you jumping up and down?"

Cameron felt his smile coming back at Sam's enthusiasm and made a conscious effort to brush off the hurt and jealousy he'd felt when listening in on Sam's phone conversation. "I was. I had a couple of hours to calm down since then," he lied.

Sam smiled, but he still looked a little confused. "Okay. I'd take you out to celebrate, but I guess you already took care of your own celebration dinner. Wait. Have you called Elena yet?"

Cameron shook his head. "I wanted to tell you first."

"We need to call her, then. She'll never forgive me if I don't let her know the second I do."

The phone call with Elena made Cameron feel a little better. Her screaming and carrying on, on the other end of the line, made him laugh, and both brother and sister insisted on taking him out for another celebration dinner together the next night, when she was free. Cameron agreed reluctantly, knowing how much both of them had already spent on him in the months he'd been staying with Sam, not even including the hundred and fifty dollars the test had cost and all the bus money and spending money Sam had given him here and there.

That night, after an admittedly fantastic dinner, Cameron couldn't sleep. All he could think about was Sam's phone conversation with Ryan, and if he was ever going figure out how to make Sam see him as a man and not a boy. Even though he finally had his certificate and that hopefully meant he had a better shot at getting a job, it was going to be a long time before he was anywhere near the same point in his life Sam was. Based on his current financial outlook, even his debt to Sam and Elena seemed overwhelming, let alone what it would cost to find his own place and pay for classes. He was beginning to feel like he was doomed even before he started.

THE FOLLOWING weekend, Cameron's anxiety and shame over the whole money situation reached a new high, when Sam turned around suddenly, before getting into Ryan's car, and hurried back to him, pulling out his wallet and handing over a couple of twenties. "Almost forgot. This isn't much, but there's plenty of food in the house, and if you need more money while I'm gone, call Elena, and she'll come down and help you out, okay?"

Cameron could feel the eyes of the three men in the car on them as he reluctantly took the bills from Sam's hand, and his face heated in shame.

"You have my number, if you need me. Be good," Sam said before turning and heading back to the car.

As Cameron watched Ryan's car pull away, with John in the passenger seat and Sam and Stefano in the back, heading to Ryan's cabin in the mountains for a weekend together, Cameron wished with all his heart the ground would open up and swallow him whole. When the car was out of sight, he went inside and paced the living room like a caged animal, fighting tears and the irrational urge to break something. Eventually, he ended up on the couch with his head in his hands and his eyes closed, breathing like Dr. Wingate had taught him. It helped calm the storm inside him a little, but it didn't wipe away any of the jealousy and shame. And as his anger dissipated, it was replaced with a gnawing fear that he'd never be able to get his shit together before Sam found someone else to fall in love with.

He had no doubts Sam and Stefano would fuck that weekend. The knowledge hurt, but not nearly as much as the fear they might actually do more than fuck, that they might discover they really liked each other and maybe even start dating when they got back. Sam was an old-fashioned guy. He'd made that painfully obvious in the first weeks after Cameron moved in. And Cameron knew he wouldn't simply hook up with a guy without developing feelings for him. The thought made Cameron clench his jaw so tight he was afraid it might crack. He had to get out of the house and do something, or he'd go crazy.

As he sat at the bus stop and tried to figure out where the hell he was going, a thought popped into his head that wouldn't let go: money. It was all about money and being able to show Sam that he wasn't a kid who needed to be taken care of.

In the past year, since his mom and Art had kicked him out, he'd done everything he could to make it on his own, *without* touching his father's guilt money, but it was taking too long to get his shit together. He needed money *now*, and the guilt money was his by right. In a sick and fucked-up way, he'd earned it, so why shouldn't he have it when he needed it? All the reasons why he'd promised himself he wouldn't use it crumbled under the weight of his fear that he would lose Sam if he didn't start showing the man he could take care of himself, and Cameron made up his mind.

As much as his stomach tried to tie itself in knots at the very idea of what he intended to do, Cameron ruthlessly forced his anxiety down, climbed onto the bus when it arrived, and headed for his mom and stepdad's house. The trip took forever, over two hours, and Cameron nearly talked himself out of it a dozen times as he changed from bus to train and back again, but he didn't turn around. This might be his dumbest idea yet, but he had to do something, and this at least had the *possibility* of being more constructive than another night partying with his friends.

When the last bus finally stopped, he forced himself to get off and concentrated on putting one foot in front of the other as he walked the last several blocks north of Wilshire Blvd, to the manicured splendor that was his mom and stepdad's prized bit of Santa Monica real estate. It was early in the evening on a Friday. The sun was warm, the weather as beautiful as it always was, and luckily, his stepdad's car wasn't in driveway. Even so, Cameron's hands were shaking when he rang the bell, so he clasped them behind his back as he waited for his mom to answer the door.

She wasn't happy to see him. That was pretty obvious by the look on her face. But she stepped out of the way, allowing him inside, and Cameron followed as she led the way into the den. She had her usual tumbler of clear liquid on ice in her hand. It wasn't water, and he wondered how many she'd had already. He'd been away too long to be able to gauge it by the way she looked.

"Arthur will be home any minute," she said without preamble, and then finished what was left in her glass in one swallow.

As always, the old hurts threatened to surface, but there was plenty of anger there too, and Cameron let the anger win, hoping it would keep him strong. "Good, then we can all have a family chat when he gets here," he said, sounding braver than he felt.

His mother's lips twisted into a grimace. "Why are you here, Cameron?"

"Why else, Mother? I want the guilt money. Oh, and I'm doing fine by the way. Thanks for asking."

Her face froze, and she turned and headed out of the room, making a beeline for the liquor cabinet on the far wall of the great room. Cameron followed and, with his arms folded protectively over his chest, sat on the back of the immense, custom-made B&B Italia couch that dominated the huge space, while she poured herself another glass.

When she simply continued to drink from the glass, without turning around or saying anything, Cameron fidgeted uncomfortably until he finally ran out of patience. "Look. The guilt money is mine. Even though I'm not allowed free access until my twenty-first birthday, it's there to help me do whatever it is I want to do with myself, and I need it now to live on and to try to go back to school."

She turned around to face him and pursed her lips. "I'm sorry, Cameron, but I don't agree. Your behavior has shown you can't be trusted with that kind of money. I know where you went when you ran away. I know about all the parties and the drugs and the... *sex*." She grimaced on the last word, and Cameron couldn't really blame her. He didn't want to think about *her* having sex either. But just because he couldn't blame her, didn't mean he wasn't pissed.

"Ran away? You mean after Art kicked me out?"

She frowned at him and shook her head. "Don't be so dramatic, Cameron. No one kicked you out."

Cameron stared at her for a few seconds with his mouth open, wondering if she actually believed what she was saying. "You mean, 'get the fuck out of my house and don't you ever come back, you piece of shit' was Art's way of saying we needed to have a heart-to-heart?"

"Watch your language," she said sharply, and Cameron couldn't help but roll his eyes. "The point is, you aren't responsible enough to handle your own finances. If we give you any of it, how are we to know you won't just waste it all on drugs?" She turned away from him and downed more of her drink before continuing in a calmer, almost wheedling voice. "If you'd decided to perhaps sign yourself into a clinic or asked for the money for another therapist, maybe. We'd work something out with paying those bills directly. But I'm not just going to hand you cash and watch you throw it away."

Cameron gritted his teeth to keep from screeching at her. After a couple of calming breaths, he said, "I'm not throwing it away. I told you. I need it to pay off my living expenses, *outside* of this house, just like Artie wants. I want to try and take some college classes, and there are some very nice people I've been mooching off who I'd like to pay back. I never once asked you for *my money* when I was with Sean. Not once. And I already told you I wasn't with that crowd anymore, when I called you after my birthday. No parties, no drugs. If you'd actually come to visit me when I texted you about where I'm staying now, you'd know that."

His mother's hand shook as she reached for her glass again, and Cameron felt a little twinge of worry despite his anger. All that booze would kill her eventually, and he didn't want that, no matter how ugly things got between them. She set her drink down and opened her mouth to say something, but the sound of the front door opening made her to stop and reach for her glass again.

Cameron felt his gut clench as his stepdad's heavy footfalls echoed off the marble tiles and faux columns in the front hall.

"Celia? I'm—what is he doing here?" Arthur said as soon as he stepped into the room.

Cameron's heart rate kicked up, and he could feel his palms starting to sweat as he stood up to face his stepfather. Arthur Cobb was well over six feet tall, with broad shoulders and powerful arms that strained the sleeves of his custom-tailored business suit. The years had added quite a bit of thickness to his middle, but the rest of him was just as hard as it looked in the college football photos that hung on the man's home office walls. He'd always intimidated Cameron, from the first day they'd met—when Cameron was a skinny twelve-year-old boy with absolutely no interest in sports—and relations between them had never improved.

*It's* my *money. They have no right to keep it from me.*

Cameron repeated those words in his head as he started his breathing exercises again. God, he wished he'd taken one of his few remaining Xanax before he'd left the house. They were buried in the bottom of his backpack somewhere, and he'd forgotten about them until that moment.

"I'm here for some of my guilt money," Cameron said. His voice sounded thready to his own ears, and it broke a little on the last word, but he held his head high and kept his back straight.

His mother and stepfather shared a look Cameron didn't understand, but whatever it said wasn't good, because Art frowned at him. "And what was your mother's answer?"

Cameron clenched his teeth. "She said I couldn't be trusted with it."

"Well, there you go. You have your answer," he replied with a sneer.

Cameron lost it. "Fuck that! It's my goddamned money! It's supposed to be used to take care of *me!*" Cameron yelled.

"Watch your language!" his mother shouted from behind him, and Arthur took a couple of menacing steps toward him.

"You watch how you speak to your mother, you hear me!"

"I wasn't talking to her. I was talking to you, since you seem to be the one pulling her strings while she drinks herself into an early grave!" Cameron shouted back.

In hindsight, that wasn't the most constructive thing he could have said, but he was beyond being reasonable at that point.

Art's face turned red, and he closed the distance between them fast. He grabbed Cameron by the upper arm and all but dragged him through the house and out the front door. "Don't come back until you're willing to apologize to me and your mother," he said. He glanced up and down their perfect street, and then he leaned in really close and hissed, "You're a fucked-up little shit. You always have been. No amount of money or therapy is ever going to fix that. If I see you here again, I'm calling the cops." Art gave him one last shove before storming back into the house and slamming the door.

Cameron wanted to scream and scream at the house until the whole neighborhood knew all of his family's dirty little secrets, but the thought of having to call Sam to bail him out when he got arrested stopped him. He walked stiffly back to the bus stop and plunked down on the bench. After taking a few minutes to get control of himself, he pulled out his phone and stared at it for a long time. He wanted to call Sam so badly, just to talk to him, to pour out every bit of his pain and replace it with Sam's voice, his kindness. But Sam was hours away, probably on a nature hike or some other shit with *Stefano*, and Cameron couldn't bring himself to hit send.

As he was about to put his phone away, it chimed and a text from Chris showed up on the screen.

*Got plans 2nite?*

He'd ignored his friend's texts for the past few days, not wanting another night of partying to feel guilty about, and look what that had gotten him—absolutely nothing but bullshit.

"Fuck it!" he said to no one in particular.

*Im all urz. Pk me up?*

# CHAPTER THIRTEEN

SAM RELAXED luxuriously in Ryan's hot tub and dropped his head back on one of the foam pads so he could look up at the stars. Stefano was stretched out in the high seat next to him, with his eyes closed, water droplets glistening on his chest and arms, and a glass of wine dangling precariously from his fingers, doing his part to enhance the gorgeous landscape around them, and Sam thought it couldn't get much better than this. He had mountains, trees, the lake, the cloudless night sky above, and acres and acres of glistening bronze skin to look at. He had good friends, good food, and good wine to share with them, and nowhere he had to be all weekend. Every once in a while, he did spare a few moments to wonder about Cameron and regret he couldn't share this with him, but right now, the mostly naked Italian next to him was making it hard to think about anything but what was right in front of him.

The night before, they'd picked up carryout at a little Chinese place in town, and they'd sat on the floor around the coffee table in the cabin's great room, drinking, talking, and laughing until well past midnight. English obviously wasn't Stefano's first language, but he was fairly fluent, and he and Sam had a good time joking about a few of the weirder Americanisms Stefano had heard since he'd moved to California. John was the only English major in the room, so he took it upon himself to defend the sometimes inexplicable corruptions of the English language, but Sam kept his mouth shut and let him at it since he wouldn't be any help in that arena.

When it was time to say good night, Sam had been pleased to discover there wouldn't be any awkwardness between him and Stefano. They'd been set up. They both knew it. But Stefano seemed to have a sense of humor about the whole thing. And luckily, the cabin had three bedrooms, so there wasn't any pressure for Sam to hop in the sack with the guy right away. Not that he was completely opposed to the idea. It had been tragically long since he'd gotten laid, and Stefano was definitely his type. But this way at least, he could take his time and get to know the guy a little first.

The next morning, all four of them went for a hike, had some lunch, and took a late afternoon swim in the lake before returning to the cabin to cook dinner. This was Stefano's first time at Big Bear Lake, and he seemed to want to soak everything in at once, with an endless enthusiasm Sam envied. That enthusiasm extended to nearly everything the man did, including making it abundantly clear, as the afternoon progressed, that he was interested in Sam for more than friendship. But for some strange reason, Sam found himself holding back, and he couldn't figure out why.

He was definitely flattered by the attention, and he was tempted—*Gawd* was he tempted—but he couldn't seem to bring himself to take that last step and initiate anything between them, even when Ryan and John left them alone together in the hot tub that night. He and Stefano were less than two feet apart, wearing nothing but swim trunks, in as romantic a setting as Sam had seen in a very long time, and he was still frozen in his spot, wondering what the hell was wrong with him.

He was pretty sure eventually the wine, his libido, Stefano's assertiveness and undeniable hotness, or a combination of some or all of those things would have won out over any of the formless reservations he had. But alas, they never got the chance. As Sam unfroze enough to reach for the bottle of Merlot perched precariously on the edge of the hot tub, he heard his ringtone coming from beneath the towel he'd left on one of the deck chairs.

Stefano opened his eyes and glanced over at him, and Sam gave the man an apologetic smile as he set his glass down and scrambled out of the tub to get his phone. He took one look at the display and frowned. "Hey, El, isn't it a little late for you to be up?"

"Sam! Sam, I need you! Shawna was in a car accident, and she's in an ambulance on the way to the hospital, and Michael is in Japan this weekend for that fucking convention!"

His sister's voice was shaky and borderline hysterical, and Sam's heart flipped. "Shit! I'm at Ryan's cabin at Big Bear Lake right now, but I'm coming as fast as I can. Is she hurt bad?"

Elena actually whimpered, a sound Sam hadn't heard since their father's funeral and hoped he'd never hear again. "I don't know. She called me right after the wreck, so I don't think it's too bad. But she sounded hurt and scared, and I'm on my way to the hospital now. Hurry, Sam."

"What hospital are they taking her to?"

"Torrance."

"Okay, I'll be there as soon as I can. Drive careful, El. I'm sure she's going to be okay, so don't kill yourself trying to get there, alright?"

Elena sniffled and blew out a shaky breath. "Yeah. Okay. Get here when you can."

Sam ended the call, grabbed the towel, and rushed to Ryan and John's bedroom door. "Ryan! I need to get back. Shawna's been in an accident."

John opened the door a few seconds later, wrapped in a sheet, and Sam could see Ryan digging through a pair of shorts on the chair behind him. When Ryan pulled his keys out and walked over to hand them to Sam, he asked, "Do you need us to come with you?"

His friend was completely naked, and judging by his flagging erection, Sam had definitely interrupted something. "No. If I can just borrow the car, I'll bring it back tomorrow."

"Are you sure? Maybe you shouldn't be driving. We can be dressed in just a sec," John said.

"I'll go with him," Stefano said from behind him, and everyone turned to look at him. The guy had already put on a pair of flip-flops and a T-shirt over his swim trunks. "Come, Sam. You are upset and should not be driving all that way by yourself. I am ready, we can go now."

Sam felt his shoulders droop in relief and gave Stefano a grateful smile. He gave John and Ryan a quick hug and hurried off to throw on a shirt and shoes as well.

The two-hour drive back to LA seemed to take far too long, and even though Stefano did everything he could to keep Sam calm and reassure him, by the time they got to the hospital, Sam was a wreck.

They found Elena in the waiting room closest to the ER, and the second she spotted them, she was on her feet and flew into Sam's arms. "Oh God, Sam. I'm so glad you're here."

"Have you heard anything?"

"Yeah, they took her in to X-ray not too long after I got here. She's got a broken wrist and a broken leg, as well as a probable concussion. They're doing some scans now, to make sure it isn't more serious than that, but they think she's going to be fine. I'm sorry for panicking and making you come back like that."

Sam shook his head and pulled her into another hug. "Don't be. I would've come anyway. But I'm glad it isn't anything more serious."

He gave his sister another squeeze and a kiss on the cheek before stepping back and lifting a hand to draw Stefano closer. "El, this is Stefano. He kept me from going crazy on the drive back."

Elena laughed and wiped at her cheeks. "It's very nice to meet you. I'm sorry I ruined your weekend."

Stefano shook his head. "Don't be silly. Family is important, and there will be other weekends."

Elena looked back and forth between them for a second, but apparently she was too wrung out to give Sam any shit, so she gave them both a tired smile. "Well, thank you for coming with Sam anyway," she said.

"El, do you want me to get you some coffee or something?" Sam asked, as his sister seemed to wilt a little more with each second.

"Coffee? Oh God, yes."

It was after midnight, but Sam had a feeling they might be there a while, so he took Stefano with him and went in search of something hot and caffeinated. As they walked, Sam decided it would be best to send Stefano home. All they'd probably be doing for the next few hours was waiting, and El didn't really look up for company. Sam pulled Stefano into a secluded corner, gave him a long "thank you" kiss good-night. Stefano's lips were lush and warm, and Sam was definitely regretting whatever had stopped him from jumping the man earlier by the time they broke apart.

Sam sighed regretfully. "Thank you so much for coming, but I think Elena would be more comfortable if it was just me right now."

Stefano nodded. "I understand. But I can come back to give you a ride home if you like."

"Thanks, but I'll probably drive Elena and Shawna home in her car in case she needs help getting Shawna inside. Go home and get some sleep. I'll give you a call tomorrow, okay?"

Stefano looked like he wanted to argue, but eventually he nodded. Sam didn't say it out loud, but he was thinking this way Stefano could head back out to the cabin as soon as he wanted to and enjoy the rest of the weekend for both of them, since there was no way Sam would be leaving town again until he was sure his sister and niece didn't need him anymore. Stefano gave him one more little peck on the lips and left, and Sam watched him go for a few moments before continuing his search for coffee.

The nurse came and got them an hour after Sam returned with the coffee. Shawna had temporary casts on her left wrist and her left leg, as well as a goose egg just inside her hairline and various other bruises and scratches. Her car had been T-boned by a guy in a Lexus RX who'd run a red light, and airbags can only do so much. She looked groggy and in pain but still in one piece, and when she gave them a tired smile, both Sam and El were finally able to relax.

The doctors released her a couple of hours later, after they'd had a chance to look over all her tests and determine that she wasn't in any immediate danger. Sam tried to call Cameron on the drive back to his sister's place, but the kid never answered, so, after they got Shawna inside, Elena told him to take her car back to his place and bring it back with him when he came to check on them, after he'd gotten some sleep and a change of clothes at his place.

By the time Sam made it home, it was almost four in the morning, and he was beyond exhausted. Some barely functioning part of his brain noted that there was an unusual number of cars on the street outside his house, but he was too tired to make any sense of it until the beer bottles and trash strewn across his yard finally registered.

"Oh, fuck no," Sam said, anger slowly clearing the fog of exhaustion in his head as he yanked open the door.

The smoke hit him like a wave. Cigarette smoke, shisha smoke, and an underlying hint of something far less legal, unless everyone in the room was carrying a prescription. There were beer bottles, cups and plates, and various other bits of trash on nearly every flat surface. There were barely conscious and completely unconscious bodies draped over all of his furniture and his floor. But even more important than what he saw, was what he didn't, like his Xbox, his TiVo, and his stereo system. The second Sam realized those items were missing, his stomach plummeted, and his eyes swung to the corner of the room where his dad's guitar was supposed to be. The stand was there, but the guitar wasn't.

"Oh no," he whispered as bleary eyes and tousled heads lifted to look at him from various places around the room.

Sam rushed the rest of the way inside then, and went from room to room, hoping someone had only moved the guitar. It was a cheap, ratty old thing, hardly worth the effort of stealing it. When he made it all the way back to his own bedroom without finding it, and found Cameron and some stranger naked and asleep in his bed instead, a tide of emotions swept over him. Rage, hurt, disappointment, and loss were only a few of the ones he could put a name to. If there were others, he wasn't ready to face them yet.

Without a word, he walked out of the house and over to his car— ironically the only thing that *hadn't* been stolen—and he pulled out his phone and called the cops.

It took a while for anyone to show up, and Sam waited, sitting on the hood of his car and watching kids stumble out of his house in ones and twos, as they made their way to their own vehicles. He watched them go, but none of them carried a guitar or any more of his electronics, so he didn't even try to stop them. The fewer kids left in his house when the cops got there the better, especially if any of them were underage. Sam didn't even want to think about getting cited for "hosting" an underage drinking party, on top of everything else.

By the time the cop car pulled up and the officers went inside to flush the last of the partygoers out of the house, there were only a few people left. Luckily none of them had any drugs on them, and all except Cameron were over the age of twenty-one. Sam gave his statement to the officer who came to talk to him as the man's partner talked to Cameron and the last of the kids who'd trashed his house. He could feel Cameron's eyes on him from time to time, but he didn't turn to look. He was too angry. At least Cameron's laptop had been stolen too, so the cops didn't really think he was in on it. Sam was relieved he wouldn't have to tell Elena the kid had been arrested, on top of everything else.

He could barely keep his eyes open by the time the officer said, "I think that's everything, Mr. Powell. We'll file the report, and you may receive a call in the next day or so, if the investigator has any more questions. You should be able to get a copy for your insurance company by next week. Do you need us for anything else this morning, sir?"

Sam shook his head. "No. Thank you for your help."

He could tell by the officer's tone the likelihood of him recovering any of his stolen belongings was pretty slim. The man gave him a sympathetic smile, collected his partner, and drove off, leaving Sam and Cameron standing on the front lawn as the sun came over the horizon.

Sam turned and shuffled toward the house but stopped when Cameron came after him. "Sam, I…."

Sam lifted his hand. "I don't care, Cameron. I'm done. I'm going to bed now. When I wake up, I want you gone. Get your stuff and go to one of the shelters El talked to you about, or find a place to stay with one of those people you invited to my house. I don't give a shit. I just don't want you here anymore."

111

Cameron stared at him, with his mouth hanging open and his eyes wide, for several seconds before he said, "Sam, *please*." There were tears in Cameron's pretty hazel eyes, but Sam was too numb to be affected, for once.

"No. I mean it. I'm done. You're one person with me and someone completely different whenever I turn my back. I don't know if you're lying to me, or to yourself, or what. But right now, I don't care. Pack your shit and get out."

He turned his back on Cameron then so he wouldn't crumble under the pathetic look the kid was giving him, and slowly he made his way back to his bedroom. Once inside, he locked the door, stripped the sheets off the bed, and kicked off his shoes before collapsing on top of the mattress with only his comforter to curl up with.

The clock by his bed showed one thirty by the time he opened his eyes again, and the only reason he woke up then was because his phone was beeping at him. There were three text messages waiting for him: one from Ryan, asking for a status update, one from Stefano, telling him he was on his way back to the cabin and to give him a call when he was up, and one from Elena, checking in. Sam groaned as he slowly got to his feet. His bedroom still smelled like cigarettes and sex, reminding him of the colossal disaster that was currently his house… and Cameron.

"Fuck," Sam said to his empty room, and he flopped back down onto his mattress and covered his face with his hands.

He'd kicked Cameron out. He'd actually done it, knowing full well the kid had nowhere good to go. There was a voice in his head telling him he'd had every right to do it. He'd left Cameron alone for a day and a half, and his house was trashed, and his dad's guitar was gone, along with most of his electronics and any other valuables he had. But his heart was giving him the same speech he'd given Ryan about how Cameron was just a mixed-up kid, and what would happen to him once he was back out there on his own?

Sam reluctantly pushed himself upright again and climbed to his feet. He unlocked his door and made his way down the hall, part of him hoping Cameron had ignored him, but a quick search showed that the kid had taken him at his word. Cameron's bag and backpack were gone from the guest room, and the dresser drawers and closet were empty. Any hopes the kid might have packed but was still hanging around, hoping to talk to him before he left, were dashed when Sam made his way to the kitchen and found the house completely empty, except for the piles of trash everywhere.

At least whoever the thieves were, they hadn't bothered to steal his coffeepot. Sam cleaned it out and got it running before making his way outside to see how bad the backyard looked. He surveyed the small space, absently noting the discarded bottles and cans and the trampled flower beds, while he tried to reconcile all his conflicting emotions. The only thing he was completely sure of was he was tired, in body and in spirit. The emotional turmoil of the last twenty-four hours had drained him dry.

He finished his second cup of coffee—out on the back porch because his house stank and his couch had several unidentified stains on it now—and took a long, hot shower, before he finally felt revived enough to pull out his phone. He sent a text to Ryan, telling him Shawna was going to be fine and asking him to relay the message to Stefano and John, promising to call later that night. He texted Elena and promised he'd be by in an hour or so. And then he stared at his phone for a long time before breaking down and texting Cameron.

*We need to talk.*

He waited a couple of minutes, but when there was no reply, he put the phone in his pocket, finished getting dressed and headed out to take El's car back to her and check on his niece.

Shawna was a little perkier after she'd gotten some rest, but the bruises looked much worse and the pain meds made her a little loopy. She had an appointment with a specialist Monday morning, and Elena said they'd know if she was going to need surgery on her wrist or not and how long she'd need to wear a cast on her arm and her leg after that. Sam offered to go with them, but El said Michael would be back by then, so they'd be fine.

When Shawna went for a nap, Elena drove him home, and on the way, Sam finally told his sister what he'd come home to and that he'd kicked Cameron out. She was quiet for a while, clearly absorbing the information as she navigated the warren of streets leading to his little neighborhood. The news of the loss of their father's guitar clearly hit her as hard as it had Sam, but her first question didn't surprise him.

"You texted him this afternoon?"

"Yeah."

"What are you going to say when he calls you back?"

"I have no idea." He laughed when he said it, even though he was completely serious.

Elena sighed. "I'll try and call him when I get home, to see if I can get him to tell me what the hell is going on with him. I'm so sorry, Sam. I never thought he'd do something like that, particularly after he'd done so well on the test, and it seemed like he'd finally gotten his act together."

Sam closed his eyes and dropped his head back against the headrest. "I know. The more I think about it, the less sense it makes. But what he did at my birthday party didn't make much sense either. I was at the end of my rope this morning, and I feel guilty for kicking him out, but I don't know if I can trust him enough to let him back in my house again either."

She nodded. "I understand. Maybe, once one of us talks to him, we can figure something out. I know deep down he's a good kid."

Sam wanted to believe that too. He *had* believed it. He just wasn't sure if he still could.

They pulled up in front of the house, and Elena came inside to have a look around.

"*Ay Dios mío.*"

"Yep."

She wandered around a little before turning back to him with a pained look on her face. "I have to get back to take care of Shawna, but if she's getting around well enough tomorrow, I could try and come over for an hour or so to help you clean up."

Sam shook his head and gave his sister a quick hug and a push toward the door. "Don't worry about it. Take care of my niece. I'll take care of this."

Elena wanted to argue. He could see it in her face. But concern over her daughter won out, and she finally nodded. "Okay. If you need to hire someone, let me know. I'll pay half. It's the least I can do."

They kissed and hugged once more before Elena drove off, leaving Sam alone in the wreck of his house. By the time the sun went down, Sam had all of the trash and the recycling picked up and bagged. He'd left the windows and doors open all day to air the place out, and he'd written a long list of cleaning supplies he was going to need to repair the rest of the damage. He was still tired, though, so after he'd hauled the last bag of trash to the street, he called it quits for the night and curled up in his bed with his laptop to get caught up on e-mails. Thankfully, he'd taken the thing with him to the cabin, and Ryan and John had stopped by briefly on their way home to drop off his stuff, or he wouldn't have even had that much. Sam was sure Ryan had been dying to tell him "I told you so" as his friend had examined what was left of Sam's house, but he'd taken one look at Sam's face and changed his mind, for which Sam would be eternally grateful.

By the time Sam was ready to go to sleep, he still hadn't heard anything from Cameron and neither had Elena. He wasn't sure whether he should be angry or concerned about that, but he had to go to work in the morning, so he couldn't stay up all night waiting.

He checked his phone throughout the next day, but he never got a call from the kid. And when he talked to Elena, after Shawna's visit to the doctor, she told him she hadn't heard from him either. They were both starting to get concerned, but there wasn't much they could do about it if Cameron wouldn't talk to them.

By the time Wednesday morning rolled around, and he still hadn't heard from Cameron, Sam had moved past most of his anger, and all that was left was worry, especially when he walked out the door to head for work and found a small bag on his front step with a folded piece of paper attached to it, bearing his name.

*I'm so sorry, Sam. I can't tell you how much. I
didn't plan it, any of it. I swear. I never wanted to let any
of my friends even know where you lived. But I got
wasted, and I let them drive me home Saturday morning,*

*and when they found out I was alone for the weekend, all these people started showing up that night, and things got out of hand. It's all my fault, and I'm trying to fix it, but this is all I could find so far. I'll keep trying and hope that you can forgive me someday.*

*Cameron*

Inside the bag were two bracelets and a watch. The watch was an old one Sam had never bothered to throw away, and the bracelets were ones Elena had made for him at Girl Scouts, when Sam was about six years old. All three had been in his dresser drawer forever, and he hadn't even realized they'd been stolen.

"Damn it, Cameron," Sam said as he stuffed everything back in the bag, closed and locked his front door, and headed off to work.

He waited until after nine to call his sister, so he wouldn't wake anyone up, and she was as concerned as he was when he filled her in.

"Sam, we really need to find him before he gets in worse trouble. None of that stuff is worth getting himself hurt over," she said, echoing his own thoughts.

"I know. I just don't know how. I don't know who his friends are. I guess I can try the cops, but he's an adult, and he left on his own, so I don't know if they'll give me any of the names from the police report."

"I have an idea," she said after a moment. "I'll try his mom. Cameron said she was fairly useless, but she pays for his cell. She might have the tracking on. I know I do for Shawna. It was part of our agreement when we got her the phone. It's worth a shot anyway."

"You have her number?"

"Yeah, I made Cameron give it to me when he first showed up on my doorstep. I wanted to give the woman a talking to, but she wouldn't speak to me then. I'll get her to talk to me now, if I have to show up on *her* doorstep to do it."

"You want me to do it?"

"Naw. It might go over better coming from me."

Cameron's mom finally called Elena back after a couple of days, and his sister managed to get the woman to agree to let Sam use her phone to track her son. Elena wouldn't tell him how exactly she managed it, but from the way she sounded on the phone, Sam wasn't sure he really wanted to know.

He met Cameron's mother after work on Friday at a coffee shop halfway between their two houses. Sam could tell the minute he saw her exactly where Cameron had gotten his looks. The woman was stunning, or would have been if years of drinking hadn't taken its toll. Her pouty lower lip, pixie-like pointed chin, and high cheekbones were a perfect match for Cameron's, but her skin was dull and splotchy under her thick foundation, and Sam was pretty sure her dark sunglasses hid a pair of eyes that wouldn't be anywhere near as bright or clear as Cameron's.

The woman barely spoke one word to him as she handed over the phone. But before she left she said, "Wherever Cameron is now, he's been there for a couple of days. You can ship me the phone when you're done." Then she turned her back on him and walked away, without giving Sam a chance to say anything other than "okay." At least the phone had a full charge, and Cameron appeared to be less than a half-hour away, even during rush hour.

Traffic sucked, as usual, but Sam eventually arrived in front of an average-sized bungalow in Inglewood, similar to his own. This one was a bit more run-down than his and had the worst yard in the neighborhood, but it didn't exactly look like a den of thieves or anything. Sam actually started to relax a little, but that didn't last long when a tweaked-out fifteen-year-old let him in and he found Cameron sitting on the floor between some guy's knees, with huge bags under his eyes and bruises on his arm and his cheek.

"Cameron?"

Cameron shot up off the floor the second he spotted him. "Sam!"

Sam took one look around him, at the grubby walls and carpet, beat-up, secondhand furniture, the hollow-eyed gaze of the kid who'd answered the door, and Cameron's exhausted, unhappy face, and he made up his mind. "Get your stuff. We're leaving."

117

Cameron stared at him for a few seconds, as if he didn't quite believe what he was hearing, so Sam softened his expression and lifted a hand to him. "Come on. Let's go home."

Cameron made a move toward him, but the guy who'd been sitting behind him on the couch stood up suddenly and put a proprietary hand on his shoulder. "Who the hell are you?"

Sam growled, but Cameron shrugged out of the guy's grip and stepped away from him, his eyes only on Sam. "Home?"

Sam didn't take his eyes off the other guy, but he nodded. "Yeah. Go get your stuff. I'll wait here."

Out of the corner of his eye, he saw Cameron spare one brief glance at the guy behind him before rushing off down the hall to Sam's right.

"Cameron!" The guy yelled after him before turning back to Sam. "Who the fuck do you think you are?"

The guy had puffed himself up a little and taken a couple of steps forward, but Sam wasn't really worried. He was tall but mostly skin and bones, his pupils were blown wide from whatever he'd been smoking, and his brain didn't appear to be firing on all cylinders. Sam was pretty sure he could take him in a fight, especially the way he was feeling at the moment, with the image of Cameron's bruises still crystal clear in his mind.

Sam kept his voice calm and quiet. He didn't want things to get ugly unless they really had to. "I'm a friend of Cameron's, and I'm here to pick him up. That's all."

Bloodshot dark-blue eyes stared back at him uncomprehendingly for a few seconds, and Sam felt like rolling his. "Why does Cam need to be picked up?"

*Oh, I don't know, maybe the fact that he looks like he hasn't slept in days, or showered, or the bruises… also the fact he's in a house full of wasted kids, and all I see is empty fast-food containers, cans of Monster, and bags of junk to eat.*

Sam didn't say any of that out loud, though. He simply wanted to get Cameron out of there, and he was pretty sure any or all of those observations would be wasted on the guy frowning down at him.

Cameron came back and grabbed Sam's arm, before he could think of what else to say, and dragged him toward the door.

"Thanks, Drew, for everything. I'll call you," Cameron called out over his shoulder as he hurried out the front door and over to Sam's car, only letting go of his arm when they reached the street. He quickly threw his bags in the back and climbed into the passenger seat, clearly ready for them to get out of there.

"Should I be worried that you just about ran out of there?" Sam asked as he climbed behind the wheel and started the engine.

Cameron shrugged and gave him a sheepish half smile. "Probably not. Drew just has a temper, and I didn't want to give him a chance to get started, if I didn't have to. He's so out of it right now, it's going to take him a few minutes to realize what happened, and I'd rather be gone when he does."

"Did he do that to you?" Sam said, indicating the bruises on Cameron's arms and face.

Cameron covered his arm with one of his hands and shook his head. "No. Not exactly."

"Not exactly?" Sam's earlier concern and anger was beginning to morph into irritation as he pulled away and headed back the way he'd come.

"It wasn't his fault. Well, the fight was his fault, but it wasn't with me. We were at a party, and I was asking around about your stuff." Out of the corner of his eye, Sam saw Cameron glance at him briefly before he cleared his throat and continued. "Next thing I knew, Drew was yelling at some guy, and then they were fighting, and I kind of ended up in the middle." Cameron touched the bruise on his cheek. "Drew accidently got me in the face with his elbow when I was trying to get him out of there."

"Jesus, Cameron. I thought I was going to have to beat the shit out of someone to get you out of *there*."

Sam could feel Cameron staring at him, but he didn't take his eyes off the road. After a prolonged silence, Cameron said quietly, "Drew's okay. He just forgets that we aren't together anymore sometimes."

"Anymore?" Sam didn't know why he asked, but he did.

"We dated in high school, but we broke up a long time ago."

Sam had a feeling Cameron had been the one who'd done the breaking up, because the way that guy had been holding onto him was more than just friendly.

They were both quiet for a while after that, as Sam focused on getting them home. It wasn't until Sam maneuvered them onto the 105 that Cameron asked, "How did you find me?"

Sam reached into his pocket, pulled out the phone, and tossed it to Cameron. The kid held it up and frowned. "Whose is this?"

"Your mom's. She lent it to us to track your phone."

A quick glance at his passenger showed Cameron staring at the thing like he'd never seen a cell phone before. "My mom? Seriously?"

Some of Sam's irritation faded, replaced by sadness at the honest disbelief in Cameron's voice. After only meeting the woman for a few seconds, Sam hardly knew her enough to pass any judgments, but it was heartbreaking to think a son would believe his mother cared so little about him he'd be surprised she'd help even that much. The questions were obviously rhetorical, so Sam didn't bother to answer. He finished the rest of the drive in silence, while Cameron turned the phone over and over in his palms and stared blankly out the side window.

# CHAPTER FOURTEEN

CAMERON SET his bags down by the door and followed Sam the rest of the way into the living room. He cringed inwardly at the stained carpets, dirty streaks on the walls, ruined furniture, and missing electronics, but he wanted to cry when he spotted the empty guitar stand. In all the drama of that morning, Cameron hadn't realized the full extent of the damage he'd caused.

"God, Sam." Cameron couldn't manage anything more around the lump in his throat.

"I met with the insurance adjuster yesterday." Sam turned around and looked at him. His face was blank, but Cameron could hear the hurt and disappointment in his voice. "I should get the check in a few days. I haven't had much time to deal with it this week, between Shawna and work."

"Shawna?"

Sam rubbed his face. "That's the reason I came home early. Shawna was in a car accident."

"Oh my God, is she okay?"

"Yeah, broken wrist, broken leg, and some bumps and bruises, but she'll be fine."

Cameron didn't know what to say. Guilt ate at him, thinking about everything Sam had gone through, and how he'd fucked things up.

"Go get a shower, Cameron. I'll see what I can find for us to eat, and then we're going to talk, okay?"

Cameron nodded miserably, grabbed his stuff, and headed back to his room and a shower. He didn't have many clean clothes left. Laundry hadn't exactly been high on his list of things to do over the past week. He actually wasn't even sure if Drew's house had a washer and dryer, even if he'd wanted to, so his choices were limited when it came time to get dressed again. He pulled out one of his few remaining clean shirts and grabbed a pair of jeans that weren't too dirty. He didn't bother with his hair or putting his contacts back in. He grabbed his glasses, made his way back to the living room, and stood watching Sam putter around in the kitchen as the smell of bacon filled the air.

The comfortingly familiar sights and smells had him on the verge of tears again, but Cameron clenched his teeth to stop any from falling and stepped up to the breakfast bar. "Anything I can do?"

Sam shook his head and handed him a plate with a sandwich. "It's BLTs tonight. Eat, while I make one for myself."

Cameron considered offering to make his own, but he didn't want to make any waves until he knew how far his welcome extended. He sat in silence and downed the sandwich so fast Sam gave him a funny look as he built his own. Cameron fidgeted in his seat as Sam ate his dinner, wanting the waiting to be over but afraid of what Sam would say once it was. At that point, he was willing to do anything to get Sam to forgive him.

When Sam was finally done with his sandwich, he got a glass of water and walked around Cameron to the couch. "Come on. Let's talk."

Cameron sat gingerly on the other end of the couch, experiencing a fresh stab of guilt as his hand slid over cigarette burns on the arm. He quickly moved his hand away from the spot and dropped his elbows onto his thighs, clasping his hands between his knees and chewing on his lip ring, while he waited for Sam to flip out on him.

Sam drew in and blew out a long, slow breath before he spoke. "I want you tell me what happened, Cameron. Because I really don't understand." Sam's words were soft. Cameron shouldn't have been surprised, but he was. It would have been so much easier if Sam had yelled. Then Cameron wouldn't have felt like he was drowning in guilt.

He wanted to tell Sam everything, but he just couldn't bring himself to tell the man how much it had hurt to watch him drive away with Stefano, knowing what would happen between them over the weekend. It would only make things more awkward between them if Sam knew how much Cameron wished it had been him in the back of that car. But he didn't want to lie to Sam either. He wasn't sure he could take any more guilt. So, he decided to tell Sam as much of the truth as he could.

He pulled his mom's phone out his pocket and set it on the now scratched and dinged surface of Sam's coffee table. "I went to see her, after you left."

"Your mom?"

He nodded. "I needed to talk to her about money."

Cameron glanced up to find Sam frowning at him. "I don't understand. I thought the reason you ended up with that guy Sean, and then here, was because they kicked you out. Why would you go back there now? Did something change?"

*I thought I had changed.*

He didn't say it out loud. Instead, he said, "Not really. I just wanted to start paying you guys back for everything you've done for me, and I thought, now that I had my GED, she'd see that I had a plan, and how good I was doing, and she'd help me for once."

"I guess it didn't turn out so well?"

Cameron's lips twisted bitterly. "You might say that. Dear old Art came home and kicked me out again, less than ten minutes after I got there."

Cameron felt Sam's hand on his shoulder, and he closed his eyes.

"I'm sorry," Sam said quietly. "But you know El and I don't need you to pay us back right now, don't you? We understand it's going to be a while before you're able to do that. You didn't have to go back there, especially not alone."

Cameron stood up to put some distance between the two of them, as anger and frustration—old and new—surged in him. "I know. You and Elena have been great, really great. But it's my guilt money—

*mine*! I shouldn't have to take yours, and they don't have any right to keep it from me. But every time I try to bring it up, they shut me down and shut me out."

Cameron paced the living room, feeling angrier and more agitated by the second. He'd thought about this a lot over the past week, and every time he did, it pissed him off more. "They don't want me living in their house anymore? Fine! It's their house. But the guilt money isn't theirs. It's supposed to be for me!"

He was so caught up in the pointless rant he'd already had over and over in his head he didn't hear Sam approach. But suddenly there were strong hands on his shoulders and concerned brown eyes looking down at him. "Calm down and talk to me. I don't understand. What do you mean by guilt money?"

That shut him up. Cameron stared back at Sam for a long time, not sure what to say. He wanted to be honest. Sam deserved at least that much from him. But the truth was ugly, and he didn't want Sam to see that ugliness every time he looked at him. He'd never planned to tell Sam any of it.

Cameron stepped out of Sam's reach and wrapped his arms around himself. He turned to stare out the glass doors at the porch and the backyard beyond, but he wasn't really seeing it.

"Please talk to me, Cameron. I want to understand," Sam said quietly, and Cameron crumbled.

"It's the money my dad and his lawyer put in trust for me, as part of his plea agreement," he replied, his voice sounding dead, even to his own ears.

"Okay?" Sam still sounded completely lost, and Cameron closed his eyes and hugged himself a little tighter.

"Did Elena tell you about my dad?"

"She said something about him being convicted of securities fraud or something. That he went to jail around your freshman year?"

Cameron shook his head. "The summer before, actually. But that wasn't what he was convicted of. It's just what the school was told, along with everybody else." Sam was silent behind him, waiting, and Cameron's stomach twisted. "He was convicted of sexual abuse of a minor—me," he said with as little emotion as possible, as if all of it had happened to someone else.

"Jesus, Cameron."

Part of him wanted to turn around, to see the expression on Sam's face, but he needed to make sure Sam knew it all first, that he understood. "They told everyone that other bullshit, supposedly to protect me, but I'm sure my mom just didn't want any of her friends to know. And the money was supposed to show how sorry he was, supposed to pay for therapists and anything else I needed, to fix what he broke. And now she won't even let me have that."

When Cameron could finally bring himself to turn around, he found Sam standing only a few feet away, practically vibrating with concern. And thankfully, Cameron saw no signs of disgust on his face.

"What can I do?" Sam asked. His hands were open and held out in front of him, as if he couldn't decide what he should do with them, caught halfway between reaching out and holding back. That, more than anything else, burst the dam on the tears Cameron had been barely holding back for what felt like forever. They slid down his cheeks in big, fat drops. He didn't make a sound or even try to stop them. Sam's face crumbled, and he closed the distance between them and pulled him against his chest. Sam wrapped his arms tightly around him, and when Cameron felt Sam's cheek press into his hair, he lost what little control he had left and melted against Sam, sobbing all over him.

Cameron didn't know how Sam managed it, but they ended up on the couch, with Cameron lying on Sam's chest, still weeping quietly as he held on tightly, like Sam would disappear if he let go.

"I'm so sorry, Cameron. So sorry," Sam whispered into his hair, over and over, as his hands made soothing motions on his back.

Eventually it occurred to Cameron that Sam was comforting him like he would a child, but it felt too good for him to want it to stop. He didn't care if Sam thought he was a kid, as long as he didn't let go.

Cameron cried himself out, and afterward he simply lay there, listening to Sam's heartbeat, soaking in his warmth and his scent as the man's breathing slowed. "I'm sorry, Sam. I'm sorry I'm so fucked-up. I don't want to be," he whispered against Sam's chest when he thought Sam had fallen asleep.

Sam's arms tightened around him. "Don't say that," he said gruffly. "You made mistakes, but I know you're trying to fix them. That's not fucked-up, even if you scared El and me half to death worrying about you."

"I did?" Cameron really wanted to see Sam's face, but he was afraid if he moved, the moment would end and Sam would get up.

"Mmm hmm," Sam said with a yawn.

"I'm sorry you were worried. I thought you'd still be mad at me."

Sam's tired sigh ruffled his hair. "It's over now."

Cameron waited a few moments, listening to Sam's even breaths before whispering, "Sam?"

"Mmmmmm?"

"I know I don't have any right to ask, but can we stay like this tonight? Just tonight… to sleep? I really don't want to be alone."

Sam blew out a breath, and his body tensed beneath Cameron a second before he started to get up. Cameron scrambled off of him and sat on the end of the couch, looking at the floor and mentally kicking himself for being so stupid. If he'd kept his mouth shut, Sam might have fallen asleep anyway, and he wouldn't have had to ask. Cameron clenched his jaw and stared at his hands, fighting another wave of emotion until Sam's outstretched hand suddenly appeared in front of him. He looked up sharply to find Sam smiling gently down at him. "Come on. I'm way too old to sleep all night on the couch when there's a perfectly good bed close by."

Cameron took the offered hand and allowed himself to be led to the back of the house, trying not to let his heart beat itself out of his chest. Sam let go of him as soon as they entered the master bedroom and walked to the opposite side of the bed. "You can stay in here tonight, but I have rules. We're going to sleep. That's it. If I feel any groping, or poking, or anything else in the middle of the night, I will dump your ass on the floor. Got it?"

Sam's lips quirked wryly, softening his words, and Cameron tentatively smiled back and nodded.

"You can take off the jeans and shoes, but the T-shirt and boxers stay on."

"Okay."

"Okay." Sam nodded with finality before turning his back to start undressing.

Cameron watched from underneath his bangs as Sam unbuttoned his shirt, kicked off his shoes, and dropped his pants, revealing a plain white undershirt and blue plaid boxers underneath. Cameron kicked off his shoes and stripped out of his own pants quickly, climbing beneath the sheet before Sam could see the beginnings of his erection. Sleeping next to Sam was going to be hard. He might be emotionally wrung out and physically exhausted, but he wasn't dead. There was no way he'd do anything to fuck up this chance, though, because he knew he might never get another one.

He closed his eyes and smiled as Sam spooned behind him, wrapping his thick arms around Cameron's chest and resting his head on the pillow behind him. Cameron could feel Sam's warm breath on his neck, and he could almost imagine a lifetime of nights like this. He felt safe and cared for, for the first time in as long as he could remember, and that was what he wanted to hold on to. He tried to stay awake, but the last week caught up to him all too fast, and he passed out not long after Sam started snoring softly behind him.

He was alone when he woke up the next morning. He felt a pang of disappointment when he discovered Sam's side of the bed was empty, but he took the opportunity to roll over and bury his face in Sam's pillow for a while, seeking comfort as shame began to wash over him again. He wished he could make the last week disappear and Sam would forget any of it had ever happened. He'd fucked things up ten times worse than they were already with his craziness, and now Sam knew all about his family's dirty little secret. Cameron squeezed the pillow tight and groaned at his own stupidity, even as his cock responded to Sam's scent surrounding him. How twisted was that?

A little disgusted with himself, but not surprised, Cameron was about to reach a hand down to get some relief when the sound of a throat clearing by the door startled him out of the fantasy his imagination had begun to supply. Fortunately, for the sake of Cameron's pride, if Sam noticed his cheeks flaming in guilt and embarrassment, he didn't say anything.

"Hey. I'm sorry to wake you," Sam said as he propped himself in the doorway, "But I have to get going to work. I'm it this weekend, since Cesar covered for me all last weekend. I didn't want to leave without checking in on you first."

Cameron sat up, pushed his hair out of his face, and rubbed his eyes, pulling Sam's pillow into his lap and resting his arms on it as nonchalantly as he could. "Yeah, okay."

"We didn't really cover everything I wanted to last night. But I want you to know I'm glad you felt like you could tell me what you did."

Cameron dropped his eyes, not feeling as confident about his decision to share all of that mess as he had been the night before. "You're the only person I've told, other than the cops and my shrink."

"I won't say anything to anyone. I promise."

Sam didn't have to promise. Cameron knew that already, but he smiled his gratitude while he fidgeted uncomfortably on the bed and his morning wood disappeared. They were both silent for a while until Sam cleared his throat. "Look, I really do have to go, but I want to continue this when I get back. Just… just promise me you'll stay here today and not do anything crazy like trying to track the guys down who stole my stuff again, okay? That was dangerous, Cameron."

Cameron felt his guilt come rushing back. "It was my fault."

Sam shook his head and crossed to the bed. He sat on the edge of the mattress and looked at Cameron soberly. "It's just stuff. Stuff can be replaced."

"Your dad's guitar can't."

Sam closed his eyes and sighed, and Cameron wanted to kick himself all over again for bringing that up.

"It's still just a *thing*, and I have my memories. It isn't worth you getting hurt over," Sam said as he patted Cameron's knee and stood up. "Promise to stay out of trouble today, so I can work and not worry about you, okay? And we'll talk again when I get home."

Cameron blew out a breath and met Sam's eyes with difficulty. "I promise."

"Good," Sam said with a nod and a smile as he stepped out of the room. Cameron was about to lie back down and wallow a little more in his guilt when he heard Sam shout from the front of the house. "And call Elena for Christ's sakes, so she stops worrying about you and calling me ten times a day!"

Cameron smiled until he heard the front door close, and he was left alone again to stew in his thoughts. Part of him still couldn't believe, after all the shit he'd done, Sam had let him come back. He didn't even deserve Sam's friendship, but all he could think about was how much more he wanted. What kind of person did that make him?

*How fucked are you when not only do you not understand half the things you do, but the person you see when you look in the mirror is someone you don't even like?*

Cameron closed his eyes and buried his face in Sam's pillow again, feeling shitty and overwhelmed. When he felt like he was going to hyperventilate from all the darkness swirling inside him, he shoved the pillow away and opened his eyes, picking a point on the ceiling and staring at it. Dr. Wingate had always said when he was feeling overwhelmed, he needed to pick one thing to concentrate on. It didn't have to be the biggest thing or the most important. In fact, it was better if it wasn't, if it was something small and simple.

As he stared at the ceiling and tried to calm his breathing, an image of Sam's house, tidy and neat like the day he'd arrived, popped into his head. Sam had done a lot to clean up since the party, but the walls were still dirty, the carpets and the couch were wrecked, and he'd noticed a faint cigarette smell when he'd come in the door the night before. His own clothes reeked of smoke from Drew's house, and he spared a moment to feel embarrassed about Sam having to smell that all night as he'd held him, before shoving the thought away and focusing on the one thing he'd already picked. He was still pretty tired, but if he worked himself into exhaustion, he wouldn't have the energy to think too much. That was going to be his plan, and step one was getting out of bed.

An hour and a half later, after having some coffee and cleaning what little Sam hadn't already done in the kitchen, Cameron was scrubbing ineffectually at marks on Sam's walls with spray cleaner and paper towels when his phone started ringing. It was Elena. Cameron took a deep breath and answered, bracing himself for the tirade to come. He wasn't disappointed. After making sure he was okay, she started yelling at him for making her and her brother worry about him. Then, she started in on him about the party and how disappointed and angry she was with him for doing such a thing. Ironically, instead of the words making him feel worse, Cameron actually felt better the longer she yelled at him. Sam's quiet disappointment had nearly torn him to shreds. He'd take being cussed out over that any day.

"Why, Cameron? Why did you do it?" Elena asked, after she'd finally wound down a little.

"I don't have a good answer. I'm sorry."

She sighed into the phone. "I talked to Sam this morning. He told me you went to see your mom and things didn't go so well. After dealing with her a few times myself, I think I can understand a little of what happened. But you know you could have called me, right? You know you can talk to me?"

"Yeah, I know. I was stupid. It wasn't intentional. I hope you can believe that. I didn't plan on throwing a party. All of these people just started showing up. I should have kicked them out. I know I should have."

"Yeah. You should have. Or you should have called me, once you figured out you were in over your head, and I would have come and kicked them out. If anyone knows how to ruin a good time, it's me. Just ask Shawna."

Cameron laughed like he was sure she'd intended. "Can I ask for your help now?"

"I told you, anytime."

"I'm trying to clean up here, but it's not working very well. Can you help me figure out what I should do?"

Of course Elena did more than tell him what to try. She showed up and took him to the grocery store. They got a few different kinds of cleaners, some little white sponges that were supposed to be magic, and rented a carpet steamer with upholstery attachments for Cameron to try on the rugs and the couch. After they got back to Sam's, Elena showed him how to use all the stuff, helped him out for a couple of hours, and then left him to do what he could, promising to come the next day to take the steamer back, if he needed her to.

Cameron worked all day—steaming everything he could steam, washing curtains and bedding along with his clothes, and scrubbing the walls. He might have to volunteer to paint the walls since the magic sponge wasn't completely successful in removing all the dings and scrapes, but the house definitely looked and smelled a lot better by the time Sam got home.

By late afternoon, Cameron could barely move his arms, so he decided to make a simple frittata for dinner. It was one of the first things Sam had ever taught him to cook, and Cameron liked the symbolism of that, like they were going back to the beginning. He smiled when he heard the front door open, but his smile faded a little when he heard Sam talking on the phone with someone.

"Thanks, but it was crazy at work today, and I'm beat. I'm staying in tonight." There was a pause. "Yeah, okay. Maybe next weekend? I'll call you sometime this week. Cool. Talk to you later. Oh, and Stefano? Thanks again for last weekend. You were really great, driving all the way back here with me. Yeah. Okay. Talk to you soon." Sam set his phone on the breakfast bar and smiled at Cameron. "Hey. That smells great." He sniffed some more and turned around, finally noticing the rest of the room. "Everything smells good actually. What did you do?"

Cameron pulled the frittata out of the oven and set it on the stovetop, giving himself time to paste a fake smile on his face, replacing the jealous frown that had been there a moment before. "Elena helped me get a steamer. I did some cleaning."

Sam went back into the living room and turned on the lights. "Wow, it looks great." The smile Sam had on his face made Cameron's little heart go pitter-patter when he joined him by the couch, but he shrugged and tried to play it off. "Everything's still a little damp, but most of it cleaned up pretty good."

He hadn't been able to do much about the burns in the couch cushions, but it definitely looked better than it had, and flipping the cushions over and a strategically placed throw covered up the worst of it.

Sam took a step toward him but seemed to change his mind halfway and turned to go to the kitchen, patting Cameron's shoulder on his way past. "It's wonderful, Cameron. Thank you for doing this."

Cameron watched him go for a few seconds before following. "I owe you a lot more than this, but it was a start."

Sam didn't contradict him as he pulled plates out of the cupboard and served them both a slice of the frittata. Cameron supposed he deserved that, along with the emotional torture of having Sam so close but now even further from his reach than he had been when they'd first met.

They ate next to each other at the breakfast bar for a while without talking, until Sam put down his fork and swiveled his chair to face him. "I've been thinking a lot about this since you've been gone," he said, and Cameron's stomach dropped. He put his own fork down, no longer feeling all that hungry. "And after last night and today, I'm even more convinced that I don't actually know you very well at all."

Cameron opened his mouth to argue, but Sam held up a hand. "I thought I did. But now, I think maybe I assumed I had you figured out, and I quit paying attention." Sam laughed and shook his head. "You'd think after everything that happened with Keith, I'd have learned something about communication in relationships, but apparently I haven't. El says I really suck at it, and I can't exactly say she's wrong."

The look on Cameron's face must have scared him, because Sam put a hand on his arm and rushed to say, "I'm not kicking you out again. I still want to help. But I know I can't help you unless you talk to me, unless you tell me what's going on in your head, because obviously I missed some things. And like I said, it isn't the first time I've been completely oblivious to stuff that's been right in front of my face, and I'm pretty sure it won't be the last either."

Cameron frowned. Despite the knife to the heart at the thought Sam didn't feel like he knew him at all, it kind of sounded like Sam was blaming himself, and that was just wrong. "It's my fault, Sam. You didn't miss anything." *At least not anything I wanted you to know about.* "I flipped out and did something stupid, all on my own. You weren't even there."

Sam sat back a little and knitted his brows. "But *why* did you flip out? I know you had that fight with your mom and stepdad. And I know there's a lot of history there that would fuck anyone up. I can't pretend to understand. But you were doing so great. Why didn't you pick up the phone and call me or Elena?"

The look Sam gave him was so hurt, Cameron felt like crying all over again.

"I wanted to," he said quietly, giving Sam what truth he could.

"So why didn't you?"

Cameron chewed on his lip while he thought of the best answer he could give. "You were going on a real vacation with your friends for the first time in forever, at least that's what Elena said. I didn't want to ruin it with my bullshit. I know everything got messed up anyway, but at the time, I thought going out and getting drunk was the better solution."

Sam rolled his eyes before picking up his plate and carrying it into the kitchen. "I hope we can agree that wasn't the case."

"Yeah, we can agree on that." Cameron laughed ruefully, trying to lighten the mood a little before he had another episode like the one he'd subjected Sam to the night before.

"And next time, you'll call and talk to me or Elena before you do anything else?" he said, dipping his head down to hold Cameron's gaze until Cam nodded.

"Yeah. I'll call."

"And you'll tell me when something is bothering you from now on, right?"

Cameron swallowed his guilt over the lie and nodded again, and Sam nodded as well before turning to the sink, rinsing his plate, and starting in on the small mess Cam had left on the counter. "Good. Then that's enough of that."

Cameron frowned at Sam's back. "Seriously? That's it?"

Sam sighed and looked back at him over his shoulder. "What do you want me to say, Cameron? Either I'm willing to forgive you and give you another chance to prove I can trust you, or I'm not. Beating it to death won't change what happened. It won't fix anything. And staying pissed about it takes too much energy."

"At least Elena yelled at me for a while," Cameron grumbled.

Sam chuckled. "El and I are two very different people. *Mamá*'s a yeller, but Dad never saw the point. I guess I'm my father's son, and she's her mother's daughter." Sam shrugged and went back to washing the cutting board in the sink, while Cameron sat and watched him, unsure of how to feel.

When Sam finished, he turned around and gave Cameron a gentle smile. "I'm not completely over being pissed at you. I'm not saying that. What I am saying is I'm willing to give you the benefit of the doubt. You're old enough now to take responsibility for what you do. I can't expect you to act like a grown-up if I don't treat you like one. So here I am, trying to treat you like a grown-up. I'm going to try to trust you to do the right thing and to ask for help when you need it, to be as honest with me as I am with you. The rest is up to you."

Cameron watched in silence as Sam made his way past him into the living room. "I'm beat," Sam said with a yawn. "I think I'm going to go to bed early, maybe read for a while before I pass out. I gotta work again tomorrow, so I'll see you tomorrow night, okay?"

"Okay," Cameron said numbly, as he watched Sam walk away.

"Oh and, Cameron?" Sam called out from down the hall. "I've been thinking about what you said about the money, the guilt money, and I think you're right, your mom shouldn't keep it from you if it's supposed to be there to help you out. That isn't right. If you want, maybe we should try and call a lawyer about it next week. It's something to think about anyway."

"Yeah, okay."

"Okay. Good night."

The house was silent around him after Sam closed the door to his bedroom, and Cameron was left with nothing but his own thoughts to keep him company. He was honest enough with himself to know that was never a good thing, especially when they were tumbling over themselves and scattering in all different directions. What he really wanted to do right then was cry and let Sam come and wrap him up and hold him all night again until all the bad stuff went away. But the bad stuff never really left. It was always there, and he didn't want Sam's pity. He wanted so much more from the man than that.

Cameron paced the living room for a while. With the Xbox and the rest of Sam's electronics gone, as well as his laptop, he couldn't even distract himself with a movie or play a game. Sam's laptop was in the dining room, but he didn't feel right asking to use that, especially not now. He supposed he could play a game on his phone or something, but the thought held little appeal when he was this worked up.

Eventually, when the walls started closing in on him, he ended up going out for a walk. Sam's neighborhood was surprisingly quiet that night, and all the houses looked the same in the dark, each of them with their seemingly identical tidy little yards and warmly lit windows. He knew from other walks there was a community playground only a few blocks away, so he headed there. He sat on one of the swings for a while, watching a small group of teenagers running their boards on the sidewalk, talking and laughing and goofing off. It was strange to think that had been him and his friends only a few years ago, before the partying and clubbing, and before they'd gotten into heavier shit than scoring a little weed or robbing Mommy and Daddy's liquor cabinet. Part of him wished for those early days, almost as much as he wished to skip ahead to his fantasy future with Sam.

Sam.

Cameron groaned and put his head in his hands. All he'd wanted, for weeks now, was for Sam to think of him as an adult, a grown-up, and an equal. Now Sam was saying he would try, but it was too late. Cameron had already fucked things up so much between them the man would never even consider dating him, even if Cameron were twenty years older than him. And as if that wasn't bad enough, everything Sam had done or said since bringing him back to his house had made Cameron fall even harder for the guy. He wasn't simply in lust anymore. He was in love.

How the hell was he supposed to live with Sam so close and not lose his shit again, probably fucking up even worse than he had already?

Cameron knew the answer, but he wasn't willing to admit it to himself.

He walked home and went to bed despite the fact that he hadn't calmed down any, and he was still struggling with himself when he woke up on Sunday. At least he'd decided maybe he could handle living with Sam, after convincing himself it would be kind of penance. He'd stay and do everything he could to make Sam's life easier to make up for all he'd done wrong. He'd cook all the meals, and he'd do all the cleaning and laundry. And when he got a job, he'd pay Sam rent so the guy would have some extra cash for trips he wanted to take. The promises he made himself were completely unrealistic. Altruism had never been his strongest character trait, but he had almost convinced himself he could do it and that it would be the best thing for both of them. Then Ryan's car pulled up as Cameron was collecting the last of the cigarette butts out of Sam's front yard, and reality gave him a good hard slap to the face.

"Hello, Cameron," Ryan said as he came around the front of his car and leaned his hip against it.

"Hi," Cameron said warily, lifting the little garbage bag he'd been filling in front of him, like some kind of shield.

Ryan looked at him for a few seconds through his sunglasses before pushing them up on his head and pursing his lips. "Sam told me you were back, but I couldn't quite believe it." Cameron tensed as Ryan shook his head. "Kid, you must have balls of steel to waltz back in here after all the shit you pulled. I'd be impressed, if I weren't so fucking pissed off."

Cameron didn't know what he was supposed to say, but Ryan didn't seem to need an answer. "Look, I'm not going to flip out and kick your ass or anything crazy like that. Much as I would like to, it would only make Sam feel even more sorry for you, and the idiot would never forgive me. All I'm going to do is try to appeal to whatever shred of decency Sam seems to think you possess and ask you to leave him alone before you do any lasting damage to the man."

The words hit a little too close to his own thoughts, so Cameron kept his mouth shut, no matter how much he wanted to tell Ryan to go fuck himself.

Ryan waited a few beats, but when Cameron didn't say anything, he huffed. "Sam is one of the kindest, most generous people I've ever met. He opened his home to you, a stranger, and all you've done is take what he had to give and then shit all over him. I know Sam can be a little blind to people's flaws, but he can't be that wrong about you. You can't possibly be so completely selfish you'd keep taking and taking from him, when you know you're just going to fuck him over again."

Cameron crossed his arms over his chest, suddenly feeling cold and a little sick despite the afternoon sun beating down on him. When he still didn't respond, Ryan's lips twisted unpleasantly. "Look, I don't have all day for us to stand here and stare at each other. Sam can be a little dense sometimes, but he's not stupid. He's going to figure out eventually you're nothing but a user, and his friends will make sure that happens sooner rather than later. So why don't you do us all a favor and leave now, okay? Before you burn *all* your bridges."

Cameron still couldn't say anything. If Ryan had yelled at him or gotten in his face, Cameron might have been able to fight back, but he didn't. Ryan calmly and quietly gave voice to every thought that had been running through Cameron's head, and Cameron had no words to deny the truth of them.

After waiting expectantly for a few more beats, Ryan threw his hands in the air, walked back around the front of his car, and climbed behind the wheel. He started the engine, but before he backed out of the driveway, he rolled down the passenger window and said, "The bottom line is Sam was doing just fine before you showed up, and you know he'd be better off if you weren't here. I know you know that. So try to be a little less of a selfish shit and do the right thing for once. I'm sure there's plenty of guys out there who'd be more than willing to give your pretty little ass a place to stay. Go find one."

With that last jab, Ryan drove off, leaving Cameron frozen in the front yard, holding the stupid fucking bag of trash, like it was all he had left in the world. Eventually he unfroze enough to drop the garbage bag by the door and go back into the house. He walked to the couch and collapsed onto it, still feeling sick to his stomach, and now strangely heavy, as if some huge weight was pressing down on him. He sat there for a long time, silently talking himself in circles in his head, trying to convince himself some part of what Ryan said wasn't true, but he couldn't do it. The asshole was right. Cameron probably would fuck up again. He wouldn't mean to, but he hadn't meant to the last couple of times either.

*"You know he'd be better off if you weren't here."*

Ryan's voice echoed in his head, but the thought was all his. Sam certainly wouldn't be worse off if he were gone. Ryan wasn't wrong about that either. Their relationship really was one-sided. Sam gave and Cameron took—a couple of meals and a few loads of clean laundry weren't going to change that.

After another couple of hours of going round and round in his head, Cameron finally made peace with what he had to do. He hated the fact he was giving that asshole Ryan what he wanted, and he was scared shitless doing it, but he couldn't take any more from Sam. And honestly, he wasn't sure he could emotionally handle living in the same house with someone he loved without doing something really stupid and burning those bridges Ryan had so eloquently talked about. If he left now, maybe he and Sam could possibly have something together in the future. It was a small hope, but better that than staying and ruining any chance he might ever have.

Cameron put together a baked ziti dish for Sam to heat up when he got home. While the casserole was cooking, he repacked his now clean clothes and tidied up his room. By the time the timer went off on the oven, he'd finished gathering the last of his stuff together, and he was sitting on the couch trying not to cry while he wrote a note for Sam. Soon enough, the food was done and there was nothing left for him to do but place the note on top of the aluminum foil-covered dish, set his spare key next to it on the counter, and walk out the door.

Every part of him hated what he was doing, but that only convinced him it was the best thing to do. As he waited at the bus stop, with his bags on the bench next to him, Cameron scrolled through his contacts until he found the one entry he'd never expected to use.

"Good afternoon," a woman's voice answered in clipped tones, "Sitkoff Law Group, how may I direct your call?"

# CHAPTER FIFTEEN

THE HOUSE was dark when Sam got home. That was his first clue something was wrong, but Cameron had made him a promise, so Sam tried to ignore the spike of anxiety that went through him. He walked through the door, set his bag on the ground, and turned on the light as he called out, "Cameron? Are you here?"

When there was no answer, Sam frowned and pulled out his phone. He hadn't missed any calls or texts. Growing more concerned by the second, Sam went back to Cameron's room and opened the door. It was empty, not a sign of Cameron anywhere. Sam made his way back through the living room to the kitchen, to see if Cameron had left him a note instead of texting for some strange reason, and when he saw it, sitting on top of a casserole dish, he relaxed... at least until he started reading.

*Sam,*

*I know I promised to call you, but I just couldn't make myself do it. So since I no longer have a laptop and this was too much to type into my phone, I'm writing you old school instead. I've decided that it's wrong of me to keep taking advantage of your generosity. You and Elena have been so great to me. I can't even begin to tell you how I feel about both of you. I want you to be proud of me. I know you said you were after I passed the GED, but*

*I want to show you I'm better than I've acted recently. I want to show both of us I'm better than that, and I have to do that on my own.*

*Please, please don't worry. I promise I won't go back to my friends or any of the other losers who get me into trouble. I have a plan this time, and I'll let you know when I'm settled.*

*You are truly the best friend I have ever had, Sam. I mean that.*

*Cameron*

*P.S. I'm also going to pay you back every penny I owe you, as soon as I can. I promise that too.*

"Shit! God damn it, Cameron." Sam dropped the paper, picked up his phone, and hit send. Cameron didn't pick up, so Sam tried again. On the third try, Cameron finally answered, "Hey, Sam."

"Hey?" Sam repeated incredulously, "Jesus, Cameron. Where are you?"

"At a restaurant, getting dinner."

Sam ground his teeth together to keep from yelling. "Tell me where you are so I can come get you."

"Sam, I…. Can you hold on a sec?" There was a pause, and then it sounded like Cameron was speaking to someone else. "I need to take this. I'll be back." There was another long pause and the background noise faded. "Did you get my note?"

"Yeah, I got your fucking note. What's going on, Cameron? I thought we'd figured this out. I thought we were good."

Cameron's voice was strange when he replied, and Sam couldn't tell if it was the connection or something else. "We were good, Sam. We *are* good. But I need to do this on my own."

The new tone in the kid's voice made Sam's chest hurt for some strange reason. "Why?"

Cameron blew out a shaky breath, and Sam wanted to reach through the phone and pull him into a hug. "I can't really explain it right now. I'll tell you when I get it all figured out. Please don't think I'm not grateful to you, Sam, and to Elena. Please don't think that. But I want to do this. I have to."

Sam heard the finality in Cameron's voice, telling him he couldn't convince the kid otherwise, and that made him inexplicably sad. "Where are you going to stay? How are you going to live?"

Cameron let out a breathy laugh. It didn't sound happy, and Sam's heart hurt listening to it. "I had a plan. I was going to try some shelters and look into some programs and maybe social services or something, while I looked for a job. But you came to my rescue, yet again, when I decided to take your advice and call my dad's lawyer. That's who's feeding me tonight. He's going to put me up somewhere, and he's going to find out what's going on with my trust. He'll call the bank and my mom tomorrow. I'll be okay, Sam. I promise."

Sam relaxed a little and sighed. "I can't say I understand, but you're old enough that I can't tell you what to do with your life either."

There was another slightly bitter laugh. "Thanks for noticing."

"Cameron—" Sam wasn't sure what he would have said, but Cameron interrupted him.

"I'm sorry, Sam. I shouldn't have said that. Look, I owe you so much already. Just trust me and let me do this for myself. I promise I'll call you, if I get in over my head again, okay?"

Sam sighed and rubbed his temple. No. It was not okay. But Sam couldn't really give a reason for why he felt that way, so he said, "Okay."

They were both silent for a while, neither apparently willing to hang up. Finally Sam said, "You're my friend too, Cameron. I care about you. Remember that, okay?"

Sam heard what sounded suspiciously like a sniffle on the other end of the line before Cameron cleared his throat. "Yeah, okay. I will. Thanks, Sam."

"Call me anytime."

"I will." There was another pause, and then Cameron said, "Sam, I gotta go. He's waiting."

"Okay. Bye, Cameron."

"Bye, Sam."

The call ended and Sam plopped down heavily onto one of the stools in front of the breakfast bar, staring around his tidy little house and feeling surprisingly empty. Eventually he got up the energy to reheat some of the dinner Cameron had made him. He ate it in the dining room, at his desk, while he absently scanned through his e-mails. It was where he'd had his dinner every night, for months before Cameron had come into his life, but it felt wrong now for some reason. Maybe Monday he'd try it in front of the TV instead. He could pick up a new TiVo and Xbox on the way home. He didn't really need to wait for the insurance check to start replacing things.

Feeling out of sorts and a little cranky, Sam cleaned the kitchen and went to bed early. Before plugging his phone in to charge, he looked at it for a long time. He'd have to call Elena at some point and explain to her what happened, but he had no idea what he was going to say. He wasn't sure he actually understood what had happened, so how the hell was he supposed to explain it to his sister? He decided to put it off until morning. If he called her from work, he'd have an excuse to get off the phone when she started yelling, or worse, crying.

OVER THE next week, Sam fell back into the routine he'd had before Cameron came into his life. He worked long hours, even though Cesar and the rest of his employees tried to kick him out the door on several occasions. On Saturday, he took Stefano up on his invitation to dinner. It turned out he probably shouldn't have because he wasn't very good company. Stefano asked him what was wrong several times over the course of the night, when Sam zoned out on the guy, but Sam didn't really have an answer. He ended up apologizing profusely as they said good night, but he had a feeling Stefano wasn't going to be calling him for another date any time soon. A guy like that probably had men lined up just waiting for a chance at him, and he certainly didn't have to wait for an idiot like Sam to get his act together.

Ryan bitched him out on the phone the next day for fucking up what should have been a sure thing, but when Sam didn't bitch back or even try to come up with any excuses, his friend let the subject drop.

Sam continued to text with Cameron every few days for the first couple of weeks, but the responses he received were short and not particularly enthusiastic, so Sam got the impression Cameron was giving him the brush-off. That hurt more than Sam really wanted to admit. He'd thought they'd had a lot of fun together, hanging out, playing music, cooking, and playing video games. For months, they'd spent nearly every night together, and Sam missed that. He was beginning to realize he missed a lot of things about having Cameron around.

At the end of the third week of living alone again, Sam broke down and decided to call Cameron and invite him to dinner at the house. It didn't seem like too much to ask, and he'd make sure to promise not to pressure him to stay or push too hard if he didn't want to talk. They could just hang out a little, like they had in the beginning. Sam had the whole conversation planned out in his head before he dialed, but when the line was picked up, it wasn't Cameron or even voice mail. It was a woman's voice.

"Hello, Mr. Powell," Cameron's mother said.

"Mrs. Cobb? I was hoping to speak to Cameron."

She laughed, and Sam was pretty sure he heard the clinking of ice cubes in a glass. "Aren't we all?"

Sam frowned. "I don't understand."

"Huh. I thought he would've at least talked to you. I received my son's phone via FedEx earlier this week, with a note saying he would be purchasing his own and any further communications should be sent to his father's lawyer. I don't know where my son is, Mr. Powell. And I'm guessing if he'd wanted you to know, he would have notified you himself. I would appreciate it if you would not call this number again and you and your sister would not attempt to contact me further."

The line went dead, and Sam was left staring at his phone, feeling both confused and hurt. Cameron had changed his number and hadn't even bothered to send him a message? He couldn't believe it. Why would he do that?

Sam tried to tell himself Cameron had forgotten, or he just hadn't gotten around to sending him the message yet. But when a week passed and neither he nor his sister received a single word from him, Sam had to acknowledge Cameron really didn't want them knowing how to get in touch with him anymore, and that hurt even more than his leaving had. It was right about then, as the reality that he might never see Cameron again really sunk in, Sam started to realize his feelings for Cameron might not have been as platonic as he'd led himself to believe.

He'd told Cameron he could be a little slow when it came to interpersonal relationships. He had plenty of proof of that, even before Cameron came along, in the form of his ex. Keith had apparently been unhappy and banging anyone he could get his dick in for months before he'd left, and it had taken Ryan telling him about it flat out for Sam to even realize it. Now, it was starting to look like he'd done it again.

*Fuck.*

In the weeks that followed, Sam spent plenty of nights thinking about it. He went to parties and let some of his friends set him up a couple of times, but the dates he went on only served to prove how easy it had been with Cameron. Maybe not during the bad times, but there hadn't really been that many of those, and that first one was only bad because Cameron had hit on him and Sam hadn't been ready for it. There'd been plenty of other times, good times. He'd lived with Cameron for months and spent most of his free time with him, and Sam had felt happier than he'd been in years. He'd actually looked forward to coming home every night. That should have been his first clue. The fact that he hadn't been interested in going out with his friends until he'd started taking it for granted Cameron would be there when he got home should have been his second.

He was an idiot. And now he'd missed out on something that could have been great.

The realization left him more than a little depressed, and to keep himself from going batshit crazy, rattling around in his empty house, he started going out even more often. Most of the time, he ended up at

Ryan and John's. As long as they mostly avoided the subject of Cameron, beyond the basics of what happened, everything was golden between the three of them, and Sam was able to forget for a little while how lonely and empty his house would be when he eventually had to go home.

The night of Ryan and John's annual pre-Halloween cookout started much like every other he'd spent with them since Cameron left—good friends, good food, and better drinks. Sam was actually enjoying himself, relaxing and hanging out. He'd had a long week at work so he chased away any fatigue and depression early in the evening with a pretty good buzz that he nursed throughout the night. The world was looking pretty golden through the beer goggles he was sporting so he didn't even mind it all that much when the subject of his love life was brought up yet again.

It was late in the evening, after most of the guests had gone home and John and Ryan were sitting with him by the pool in the couple's perfectly landscaped backyard. John was drunkenly trying to fix him up with another coworker at his firm, and Sam was trying to put him off gently. Even drunk, Sam knew he was done with fix-ups for a while. He needed time to figure some things out before he subjected another poor man to an evening with "mopey Sam." He'd vowed he wouldn't do that to anyone else until he felt like he was over the might-have-beens running through his head.

"Come on, Sam. You've been dragging around for weeks," John wheedled. "I mean, for God's sakes, you let that gorgeous piece of Italian man-flesh... what was his name?"

"Stefano," Ryan supplied, unhelpfully.

"Yeah. You let that one get away, without even a test drive. What was up with that?" John's eyebrows were scrunched together almost comically over his glazed blue eyes.

"Look. I appreciate what you're trying to do, but I need a little time."

"Time to what? Hang out with us every Saturday night?" Ryan asked before throwing back what was left in his tumbler.

"Way to make a guy feel welcome, thanks," Sam said, frowning at the two men who were supposed to be his closest friends.

"We didn't mean it like that, Sam. We're just worried, that's all," John said, placing a hand on his arm and squeezing. "It's pushing a year since Keith left, isn't it? How much longer do you need to get back on the horse?"

Sam shook his head and took another pull from his beer bottle. If he hadn't been drunk, he would have kept his mouth shut at this point. But he was drunk, so he didn't. "It's not about Keith, not really. It's Cameron."

Ryan scowled at him. "What about him? Don't tell me the little user came back around?"

"Don't call him that," Sam said angrily. "You don't know him. You never gave him a chance."

"It's true, Sam. Everyone saw it. He used you for months and didn't do anything in return but fuck up your house and fuck around with your friends," Ryan shot back.

Sam continued to shake his head as his temper rose, and Ryan got to his feet, making an exasperated sound.

"God, Sam! What does it take to get you to realize there are people out there who just aren't any good? Look, I'll tell you what I told him: you're better off without him. And obviously even *he* figured that out, since he left. The only decent thing he ever did for you."

Sam froze in his seat as Ryan's words started to sink in. "What you told him? You talked to him?"

Ryan abruptly stopped his agitated pacing, but he wouldn't meet Sam's eyes and John looked like he'd swallowed a bug.

"Yes. Okay? Yes, I talked to him," Ryan said unapologetically.

Sam suddenly felt sick. "When?" When his friend didn't answer, Sam stood up and walked over to him. "When, Ryan?"

Ryan chewed his lip for a second before he rolled his eyes and said, "The day he left."

"And you told him I was better off without him? How could you do that? How could you be so cruel to someone you don't even know?

Someone who...." Sam stopped there before he shared too much. Cameron's secrets weren't his to tell.

Ryan looked back at him defiantly. "Because I'm your friend, and I didn't want you hurt by some loser who was taking advantage of you. Jesus, Sam. All he had to do is bat his pretty little eyelashes at you and squeeze out a tear or two and you'd forgive him anything."

Sam clenched his fists at his sides to keep from punching his best friend in the face. When that didn't seem like it was going to be enough to stop him, Sam spun on his heels and stalked away. He wished now he hadn't had quite so many beers because he was really too drunk and too pissed off to drive home. Sam collapsed onto the couch in their entertainment room and buried his face in his hands. He sat like that for a while until the cushion beside him dipped and he felt an arm wrap around his shoulders.

"I'm sorry, Sam," John said tiredly.

"He doesn't know him. None of you really do. Not like I do. He had no right," Sam said miserably.

"My partner is an asshole," John said, and they both laughed. "But you knew that already."

Sam nodded. He didn't really have anything to add to that, and after a prolonged silence, John asked, "What's going on, Sam? I thought you'd talked to Cameron, and he told you he was doing fine. His dad's lawyer was helping him out. Why are still so worried about him?"

"I'm not. Well, okay, maybe I'm a little worried, but that isn't what's bothering me." Sam stopped there and took a deep breath. "I miss him, John. And I think I might have missed out on something great, because I was too blind to see it until he was gone."

John searched his face. "Are you saying you have feelings for him?"

"Yeah, I think so."

"Did the two of you ever...?"

147

Sam shook his head and smiled sadly. "No. We didn't. But I've been thinking maybe we should have, maybe *I* should have. Now he's disappeared, and I might never get the chance to find out."

"I'm sorry, Sam."

"Thanks." Sam took another deep breath and let it out. "I'm going to go sack out in the guest room, okay? I don't want to talk to Ryan again tonight. I might say or do something I'll regret."

John nodded. "I'll talk to him. Good night, Sam."

"Good night."

He slept for a few hours, long enough to sober up, and then he drove home. He was still angry and upset, but there wasn't much he could do about it. It was around 5:00 a.m. when he got home, so he drank a big glass of water to ward off the impending hangover and crawled into bed. It was close to noon before he got up and moving again, and he was on his third cup of coffee when Ryan came knocking on his door.

"If you're going to punch me, can we do it now and get it over with?" Ryan asked with a tentative smile, as if he wasn't sure if it was a joke or not.

Sam sighed. "I'm not going to punch you, no matter how much you might deserve it."

Ryan relaxed a little and nodded toward the living room. "Can I come in?"

Sam stepped out of the way and closed the door behind him before making his way to the kitchen. "Coffee?" he offered as he refilled his own mug.

"Yeah, thanks. I swear I'm not going to drink that much again for a very long time," he said as he slumped into one of the stools by the breakfast bar.

Sam stayed silent as he poured and handed over the mug and the cream and sugar, and Ryan gave him a pained look. "I'm sorry, Sam. I really am. If it makes you feel any better, John yelled at me a lot, and I think I might have to sleep on the couch for a while again."

"A little," Sam said.

Ryan grimaced. "Look, other than John, you're the best and the nicest guy I know. And there are plenty of people out there who take advantage of that—me being a prime example. I was only trying to protect you from someone I thought was a user."

Sam put his mug down and faced him. "But you never even tried to get to know him. You decided before you even met him you weren't going to like him and you weren't going to give him a chance, so you saw only what you wanted to see."

"Maybe." He said it very begrudgingly, and Sam got the impression his friend wasn't going to change his mind about Cameron anytime soon.

"It's more than that, Ryan. Whether you liked him or not, he was a guest in my home, and from everything I've heard, you treated him like garbage from day one. Not only was he my guest, but he was also my friend, and you went behind my back to chase him away. How could you do that?"

"I tried to talk to you about him, Sam, to warn you."

"And I told you, you were wrong."

"You told me I was wrong about Keith too," Ryan shot back, and Sam sighed.

"Look, I'm a big boy. Keith left me, and yes, that hurt. But Keith wasn't hurting and vulnerable. Keith wasn't alone and virtually homeless. Cameron was, and you still came after him. Yes, he messed up my house, but that was between me and him. He lived here with me for months, Ryan. Don't you think it's possible I might have seen a different side of him than you did?"

Ryan pursed his lips and scowled for a second. Sam tensed, waiting for him to say something nasty. But his friend showed unusual restraint and simply shook his head. "I'm sorry, Sam. I don't know what else to say."

"Promise me you'll butt out of my problems unless I *ask* you for help."

"I can promise to try."

Sam laughed and massaged his forehead. "I guess I'll take that, for now. I'm still mad at you, though."

Ryan gave him a sheepish smile. "Not the first time, and I'm pretty sure it won't be the last either. I can be a real asshole, just ask John."

Sam laughed. "I don't need to ask John."

After taking a few more sips of his coffee, Ryan looked at him with genuine concern in his eyes. "Are you going to be okay, Sam?"

Sam gave his friend a reassuring smile and glanced at Cameron's letter, still propped up at the end of the breakfast bar, next to his keys and his wallet. "Yeah. I'll be okay."

# CHAPTER SIXTEEN

CAMERON PUT his car in park, took a deep breath, and rested his shaking hands on the wheel. After a couple more steadying breaths, he reached down and picked up the envelope on the passenger seat, opened it up, and checked for the tenth time that the money was still in it. There wasn't much, but it was all he'd managed to save in the seven months since he'd left Sam's house. He had the guilt money now, what was left of it, but he didn't want to use that unless he absolutely had to, so it had taken him longer than he wanted to get enough money together to even start paying Sam back.

In a fit of nerves, Cameron pulled the visor down and checked himself out in the little mirror on the back. He hadn't bothered with makeup, remembering how Sam preferred the natural look, and his hair was too short to straighten, now he'd cut off all the black. That meant there wasn't much he could do even if he didn't like what he saw so all he was really doing was stalling.

Cameron put the visor back up and forced himself to get out of the car. As he got closer to the house, he noticed another car in front of Sam's in the carport and started to regret not calling ahead. He still had Sam's cell in his contacts, and he'd thought about calling a thousand times, but he'd talked himself out of it every time. Now he was thinking he should have at least called to make sure Sam wasn't busy.

The feeling only got stronger when he looked through the front window into the living room and saw a gorgeous blond he didn't recognize sitting on the back of the couch. The man was holding a wine glass, smiling, and talking animatedly to someone in the kitchen, and Cameron's stomach twisted. He considered turning around and running back to his car, but he stood his ground instead. Felicia, his new cognitive therapist, would be so proud of him when he told her. He squared his shoulders, swallowed his disappointment and anxiety, and knocked on the door like the big boy he was now.

Lucky for him, Sam was the one who answered the door, not the tall blond, and he looked even better than Cameron remembered. Despite the long separation and the awkwardness of the situation, Cameron felt something deep inside him unclench the second that big, welcoming smile spread across Sam's face. Cameron couldn't help it. He was still so much in love with the guy it hurt.

"Cameron! Oh my God." Sam said, and before Cameron could open his mouth to respond, he was in Sam's arms, having the breath squeezed out of him.

If ever Cameron had been worried about what kind of reception he'd receive, he wasn't now. He closed his eyes and buried his face in Sam's shoulder, not caring what it meant or that they might be being watched by the hottie in the living room. When he opened his eyes again, he saw the blond was indeed watching them, but the expression on his face was curious, not hostile. Cameron stepped out of the hug anyway. He wasn't there to cause any more problems for Sam, no matter how much he might want to, in this particular case.

He cleared his throat, and before he forgot why he was there, he held the envelope out to Sam.

"What's this?" Sam frowned as he opened it and stared at the rumpled bills inside.

"It's not much, but it's what I've saved so far. The money for the test is there and a little toward what I owe you for everything else." Cameron managed to get that out with a steady voice, but he wasn't sure how long it would last. Sam didn't look at all pleased.

"Cameron, I haven't seen or heard from you in over six months, and you show up out of the blue to give me money?"

He sounded hurt, *really* hurt, and Cameron's stomach twisted as he fidgeted nervously on the front step. "I promised I'd pay you back."

Sam stared at him for a long time without saying anything, and when Cameron glanced nervously over Sam's shoulder, the blond had disappeared.

"I thought we were friends. I guess I was wrong about that too, huh?" Sam said quietly, and Cameron wanted to cry.

"No, Sam. You weren't wrong," he said in a rush. "I'm sorry I didn't write or call. I am. I just needed some time to figure things out for myself, and I knew if I kept talking to you, I'd break down the second something went wrong, and want you to fix it for me. And you're such a great guy, you'd do it without even blinking an eye. I couldn't keep doing that. I needed to prove...." Cameron's throat closed up then, and he stopped.

"Prove what?"

"To prove I was good enough to be your friend."

"Shit, Cameron. You didn't have to prove anything to me. You *were* my friend. Did Ryan say that to you? If he did, I may have to find him and kick his ass, even though I said I wouldn't." Sam actually growled then, and Cameron laughed, stopping the flood of tears that threatened to embarrass him.

"I guess you found out he talked to me, huh?"

Sam ground out an affirmative, and Cameron smiled sadly. "He didn't say anything I wasn't already thinking, Sam. I might think the guy is an asshole, but he wasn't completely wrong."

"Yeah, actually he was."

Cameron started to argue, but Sam held up a hand to stop him. "Come inside, Cameron. Stay for dinner and talk to me. Tell me everything."

Cameron wanted to. God, how he wanted to. But the thought of the blond waiting somewhere in the house was too much. He couldn't sit down and talk to Sam with his date right across the table. "I can't, Sam. Not yet."

"Why?" The hurt and bewilderment were back in his eyes, and Cameron had to look away.

153

He took a deep breath and steeled himself. He had to be honest, if he was ever going to make any of his personal relationships work. It was something he and Felicia had spent a great deal of time on. "I don't think you understand how much it hurts me to see you with someone else. And that's my fault, for not telling you. But I can't do it, not yet. It would be better if we met for lunch or something, okay? I'll give you my new number."

Sam's eyes were wide, when Cameron finally dredged up the courage to look at him again, and the smile spreading across his face was dazzling... and confusing. Sam took a step forward, closing the distance between them, and reached up to cup Cameron's chin. "I don't think *you* understand how much I missed you," he said before he leaned in and gave Cameron a gentle peck on the lips.

Cameron drew in a sharp breath and searched Sam's face. "What about the guy?" he said, waving a hand in the general direction of the living room.

Sam smiled. "That's just Ethan. He's another old friend from high school. He and his very pregnant wife are staying with me for a few days. He wants to show her some of our old haunts, since they couldn't make it for the ten-year reunion or my birthday party, and they might not get a chance to travel again for a while after the baby comes."

Cameron continued to stare, with his mouth hanging open like an idiot, until Sam smirked at him and kissed him again. This kiss wasn't a peck. It was slow and soft. Sam took his time, teasing and learning every inch of Cameron's mouth, until Cameron was whimpering into the kiss and twisting his hands in Sam's shirt, trying to get closer. Eventually, Sam pulled back and gave Cameron an incredibly sexy smile. "I always wondered what it would be like with these," he said, running his thumb over Cameron's lower lip and playing with lip rings. "I like it. A lot."

Cameron had never seen this confident, sexy side to Sam before, but he knew he wanted to see it again and explore all the promises Sam's eyes were making, so badly, he could barely think.

Sam looked at him with such happiness and tenderness, Cameron felt like melting. Sam cupped his chin with one hand and ran the other through Cameron's hair, cradling the back of his skull. "Stay for dinner."

Cam nodded. What else could he do? And Sam grabbed one of his hands and pulled him inside.

To say dinner wasn't easy to get through would be an understatement. Sam's friends were really nice. Ethan was much more warm and friendly than Ryan had been and his wife, Veronica, was sweet, but all Cameron wanted was to be alone with Sam, doing more of what they'd started on the front porch. He could barely concentrate on what was actually going on in front of him. He also really didn't want to talk about everything that had happened to him over the last several months with strangers in the room, but Sam didn't want to wait to hear all about it, and Cameron didn't have the heart to refuse him.

"My dad's lawyer set me up in a motel until he could get a judge to grant him and his accountant access to my trust. After that, I went to the community college and talked to some people and they got me signed up for classes. It's all just basic level stuff but I should be able to move up to more serious classes in a couple of semesters. And at school is where I found the ad for my apartment. There was a note on one of the bulletin boards put up by a couple of students looking for a third roommate, and I grabbed it."

Sam had been smiling encouragingly up until Cameron said that last sentence.

"Roommates?" Sam said, frowning a little.

Cameron hid a smile as he realized Sam might actually be jealous. Part of him wanted to let the moment stretch out to see if he was right, but with Sam's friends sitting there, he didn't feel comfortable teasing. "Amber and Kaley. They were looking for another girl, but they said I was close enough, and we've been getting along really great. Amber's the one who told me about the opening at the coffee shop where she works, and the restaurant next door needed a little extra help too, so I'm working part-time at both until something full-time comes up."

"Oh. Okay, that's great, Cameron. Sounds like you've got some new friends. I'd love to meet them sometime," Sam said, his smile returning.

Sam and his friends asked him more questions and by the end of the meal, Cameron was feeling a little hoarse from talking so much. He really wanted to be done with that part. And luckily, for the sake of his sanity, Sam and his guests had been sightseeing all day, and Veronica was tired. The couple went to bed early, leaving Sam and Cameron alone to clean up and finally spend some quality time together.

The way Sam kept looking at him throughout dinner, half-hot, half-hopeful, had made Cameron feel like he was about to crawl out of his skin if he didn't get the man on the couch, or on the floor, or *anywhere* even remotely flat very soon. But even when they were alone, Sam made him wait—the bastard—torturing him with gentle touches and brushing up against him as they worked in the tiny kitchen, cleaning up. It reminded Cameron of his first few weeks at Sam's house, when he'd been trying to seduce Sam using the exact same methods. Cameron wanted to tell Sam he was a sure thing, but he supposed he deserved a little torture, and he still wasn't exactly sure where they stood. Sam had told him he'd missed him, and they'd kissed, but that was it. He was so close to getting what he wanted for so long, Cameron was afraid to make any more mistakes.

When the kitchen and dining room were finally clean, Sam took his hand and led him into the living room. He looked deeply into Cameron's eyes and said, "I missed you so much, Cam. I didn't realize it until you were gone for good, and I don't want to make that mistake again."

Cameron felt his shoulders slump in relief. Sam was nervous about screwing up too. He felt so much better now. He squeezed Sam's hand and looked up at him through his eyelashes, chewing on his bottom lip. "Does this mean I can finally have you?"

Sam laughed and the tan of his cheeks seemed to get a little darker. "Yeah. You can have me."

"Oh, thank God!" Cameron launched himself at Sam, sealing their lips together and pressing as much of himself as he could against Sam's body.

Sam laughed into his kiss, but he didn't try to get away. He only pulled Cameron closer and kissed him back until they were both breathless. "Can you stay?" Sam panted, as his hands roamed down Cameron's back to cup his ass.

Cameron ground his cock into Sam's thigh. "Hell yes," he said before licking a line up Sam's throat and nibbling on his jaw. Someone was getting fucked tonight, and Cameron didn't care who. He hadn't gotten anything but a few blowjobs and hand jobs since he'd met Sam, and his now twenty-one-year-old libido was dying for a good fuck.

Sam groaned and cupped the back of his head, holding him there. "Unfortunately, we're on the futon, since I gave my bed to the pregnant couple," Sam said, his voice hitching as Cameron bit down on his earlobe.

Cameron didn't give a shit where they ended up, as long as it was flat, and he could get Sam naked on it.

"Come on," Sam said, as he stepped back and grabbed Cameron's hand again, dragging him back to his old room. Cameron didn't bother to look around when Sam turned on the lamp by the futon. The furniture was in roughly the same place so they wouldn't trip over anything on the way to the bed. That was all he really cared about. He closed the door and waited impatiently for Sam to turn around again.

Sam was flushed and smiling as he closed the distance between them, but there was something in the man's eyes Cameron didn't like.

"Are you sure? We can slow—" Sam started, but Cameron didn't let him finish. He wrapped his arms around Sam's neck and kissed him and kept on kissing him until Sam was clutching his shirt and trying to pull it over his head. Cameron stepped back enough to get it off and kicked off his shoes, glad he'd chosen his boat shoes over his favorite pair of chucks.

He was working on his belt when he noticed Sam wasn't undressing himself—he was simply watching as Cameron did. Cameron didn't usually feel all that self-conscious about his body. He knew he was a little on the short and skinny side, but most of the guys he'd been with seemed to like that. Sam was different, though. Cameron had seen the type of guys Sam usually went for, and they didn't look like him. He'd actually tried to put on a little weight over the months they'd been apart, but he hadn't gotten very far.

He stopped undressing, with his zipper halfway down, and looked up nervously to check Sam's reaction. Sam's gaze was locked on the hands Cameron had left resting on the opening to his pants, and he only glanced up when Cameron didn't continue with what he'd been doing. Cameron saw so much heat in Sam's brown eyes he had to believe the man had a penchant for short and skinny somewhere in his libido. Lucky him. But he didn't give Sam any more time to find fault with him before he let his pants drop and pounced on him, stripped off Sam's T-shirt, and dropped to his knees to open his zipper.

When Sam's shorts were around his ankles, Cameron buried his face between Sam's legs, nuzzling his cock and balls through his boxers as he put both hands on Sam's ass and squeezed. Sam bucked his hips a little and he swore under his breath, cupping Cameron's head in his palms.

"Fuck, that feels good," Sam whispered, and Cameron grinned as he did it again.

Eventually Cameron grew impatient with the teasing and tugged on Sam's boxers until the head of his cock peeked over the waistband. Cameron rose up enough to mouth it while he pushed his hand through the opening in the front, fondling every bit of velvety skin he could reach. He looked up to find Sam watching him intently, so he made a show of tonguing the slit and rubbing the crown over his lips and chin. Sam tightened his hands in Cameron's hair, letting him know without words how much he liked that.

Cameron suddenly wanted to make Sam go crazy more than anything else in the world. He wanted to see Sam panting and desperate for him, even more than he wanted to get off himself. It was weird, but definitely hot. Cameron had the strange feeling he might even be able to come just from watching Sam lose it, and he set to work on Sam's cock to prove it, swallowing it down as he tugged the boxers out of the way, working the sensitive flesh in his mouth with every bit of skill he had, egged on by Sam's moans of pleasure.

After only a short while, Sam started trying to pull him off. "Hold up," Sam panted. "I don't want to come yet."

Cameron looked up at Sam, his mouth still wrapped around his cock, and Sam closed his eyes and groaned. "Come up here before I lose it."

Sam was serious, he dropped his hands to Cameron's shoulders and urged him up, and Cameron reluctantly let Sam's cock slip out of his mouth with a wet pop as he rose. Cameron wiped his mouth with the back of his hand and pouted. "I wanted you to lose it."

Sam smiled and kissed him. "We have all night. I haven't even gotten you naked yet, and I'm not sure my recovery time is what it was ten years ago, so humor me, okay?"

Cameron felt Sam's warm, rough hands slide down his sides until his fingers teased inside the waistband of Cameron's jeans and boxer briefs. Sam pushed inside until he had both hands firmly gripping Cameron's ass, and used his hold to pull Cameron against him. Cameron's cock pulsed as the heat and hardness of Sam's rubbed against him through the thin material, and he started to wiggle his hips, trying to get his pants to fall. Sam chuckled and helped him until they both could step out of their clothes and stretch out on the futon.

"I've had a lot of fantasies about you in this bed," Cameron confessed as he straddled Sam's thighs and ran his hands over Sam's lightly furred chest.

"Oh really?" Sam said with a sexy smirk Cameron decided he really liked.

"Uh-huh," Cameron replied a little coyly.

"Like what?" Sam's eyes were following everything Cameron did with so much intensity and heat, Cameron felt like he was going to burn up if he didn't get the show on the road pretty soon. Sam had already blocked his original plan of sucking the man until he couldn't walk, so it was back to plan A. One of them was getting fucked and soon.

Cameron smirked at Sam and said, "All kinds. There's one where I ride you like this, until we both go blind." Cameron rotated his hips and ground their cocks together to illustrate his point, and Sam's hands gripped his ass, holding him there as Sam closed his eyes and groaned. When Sam finally opened his eyes again, they were almost black, and judging by the way his cock pulsed against Cameron's, Sam really liked that idea. At least until he groaned again, this time in what sounded like frustration, and let his head fall back on the pillow.

"Fuck! The stuff's in my bedroom with Ethan and Veronica."

Cameron would have laughed at the pained expression on Sam's face if it weren't for the fact he was going to be denied as well. Sam's cock was by no means small, and Cameron had gone without for a long time. He wasn't looking forward to taking that thing without lube, although he was tempted to try. But he never fucked without condoms, no matter how wasted he got, and even though he trusted Sam with his life, he wasn't so sure Sam could trust him.

Cameron was trying to think up a polite way to knock on the couple's door to retrieve the items they needed, when Sam jolted beneath him. "Wait. Hold that thought," Sam said, as he dumped Cameron on the mattress and pulled on his boxers before peeking outside the door. The coast must have been clear because Sam looked back at him only long enough to say, "I'll be right back" before disappearing into the darkened hall and closing the door behind him.

Cameron flopped back on the mattress and let out a frustrated sigh as he waited impatiently for Sam to come back. Luckily Sam wasn't gone long, and he was carrying a small black travel case with him when he came back. "Found it," Sam whispered in triumph, waving the bag in the air, and then he froze in the middle of the room and simply stared as Cameron lay stretched out on the bed, stroking his cock and soaking up the attention.

Sam tossed the case by the bed and shucked out of his boxers again in no time. He hurried back to the bed, climbed in next to Cameron, and put a hand over the one on his cock as he took Cameron's mouth in another hot kiss. Sam spent some time kissing, and licking, and nibbling every part of Cameron he could reach, including the bars in his nipples, until Cameron felt like he would scream if he didn't get Sam inside him soon. He had no problem volunteering to bottom so they wouldn't have to waste time on that discussion. And now that he had, he was desperate for it.

Tired of waiting, Cameron rolled Sam onto his back and straddled his hips again as he reached down for the travel case. He tried not to think about the last time he'd seen that case—right before Sam had gone away for that weekend with Stefano—as he fished inside until he found the condoms and travel-sized lube. He tossed the condom to Sam and was popping the lid on the lube to get himself slicked up, when Sam's hand came down over his, forcing him to stop. When Cameron looked up at him in confusion, Sam reached up and cupped his cheek, bringing him down for a slow, tender kiss that made Cameron's chest ache with its sweetness.

"We don't have to do this yet if you're not one hundred percent sure," Sam whispered against his lips.

The look Cameron gave him must have conveyed the "are you fucking kidding me?" that was running through his head, because Sam laughed and kissed him again with more passion as he gripped Cameron's cock and gave it a few strokes. "Okay, okay. I just wanted to make sure. At least let me do that," Sam said as he took the lube out of Cameron's hand and squirted some on his fingers.

Cameron leaned forward and raised his ass. This would be a somewhat new experience for him. He hadn't been with many guys who liked foreplay as much as Sam seemed to, but he had a feeling he was going to like that fact a great deal in the future, especially when Sam started teasing around his hole, rubbing behind his balls and working him until Cameron was riding his fingers in desperation.

"God, Sam, I'm ready already. Come *on*," he whined. Sam's answering laugh sounded strained, and the man was flushed and sweating underneath him, so Cameron knew he had to be just as hot for it as he was.

Cameron pulled off of Sam's fingers, grabbed the condom, and rolled it onto Sam's leaking cock before slicking it up and guiding it to his entrance. Sam was thicker than Cameron had had before, so part of him was glad Sam took his time getting him ready. But most of him just wanted that stretch and fullness so badly he didn't care about the discomfort, and he lowered himself down onto it, faster than he probably should have.

They both gasped as Cameron came down and rested for a moment with Sam fully inside him. When Cameron opened his eyes, Sam was looking at him with such sweetness, such open adoration, he almost lost it right there and came all over Sam's chest. Something of what he was feeling must have shown on his face because Sam suddenly pushed himself up on one arm and wrapped the other around Cameron's shoulders, drawing him down for a kiss.

Sam took over for a while then, kissing Cameron deeply while he thrust and withdrew in short stokes inside him. The feeling was incredible. It was all he'd been hoping for and more, because it was Sam inside him, Sam whispering his name as he pulled Cameron close and moved in him.

At some point, Sam flipped them over so Cameron was on his back, and Sam was pumping down into him. Cameron wrapped his legs around Sam's hips then, digging his heels into Sam's ass as Sam fucked him hard. Cameron must have been getting loud in his approval of this new aggressive side to Sam, because Sam laughed breathlessly and captured his mouth, swallowing his moans and dirty words of encouragement as he pounded him even harder. It only took a couple of pulls on his cock for Cameron to shoot off between them, and Sam wasn't far behind. Cameron's whole body clenched in orgasm as Sam buried his face in Cameron's neck and pumped those last few times into him.

When Cameron came back to himself, he could feel Sam's hot breath on his neck as Sam panted in his own aftermath. Before things got uncomfortable, Sam groaned and pushed himself up, letting his cock slide free and flopping onto his back next to Cameron. "Oh my God. I think you're going to kill me," Sam panted as he tossed the condom at the trashcan by the bed.

Cameron grinned as he stretched out his legs, luxuriating in the ache of the well-fucked. "I hope not. I have lots more fantasies left."

Sam chuckled and kissed Cameron's sweaty forehead. "You're gonna have to give me a minute or two… or sixty."

Cameron rolled up on one elbow facing him and smirked. "How about twenty?"

"Do I get a nap?"

Cameron slid a hand over Sam's chest, raking his fingers through the fine dark hairs between his pecs and around his nipples as he licked his lips suggestively. "Maybe."

Sam groaned theatrically, but he didn't pull away as Cameron continued to explore him with his fingers. Sam's cock was definitely showing some signs of renewed interest, but when Cameron smiled up at him, he found Sam looking back with a strange, almost sad expression.

"What?" Cameron asked.

Sam shook his head and smiled. "I really did miss you, you know." Sam reached up and carded his fingers through Cameron's hair before letting his hand slide down to cup his cheek. Cameron melted into the caresses, closing his eyes and putting his hand over Sam's.

"I missed you too."

"Don't run away on me again." Sam's face was serious when Cameron opened his eyes again, and Cameron could see he'd really hurt Sam by doing what he thought was best.

"I won't."

Sam smiled suddenly and pulled Cameron in for a kiss. "Good. I missed having you here with me. I want you to come back." Sam's smile was so happy and his eyes so bright and hopeful, Cameron hated to bring him down, but he didn't want to lie either.

"I want to, Sam. I really do," he said, hoping Sam would hear and see how much, in his voice and in his face. But Sam obviously heard and saw the regret there too, because his smile fell a little.

"But?"

Cameron sighed. "But, I can't, not yet anyway."

Sam's smile fell the rest of the way. "Why?"

Cameron pulled away from him and sat up so he could think clearly enough to explain himself. Lying there, all curled up next to the man he was in love with, was making it really hard to think of all the reasons why he shouldn't give in. "Because I know me, Sam. I know how I am. And if I lived with you right now, it would be too easy for me to let you take care of me again. The first time something went wrong at work or school, it would be right there at the back of my head that I could quit. And I'd convince myself, and *you*, it was all someone else's fault."

"I don't believe that, Cameron. Look how far you've gotten on your own already. Besides, you're making me sound like a sap. I'm not that bad," Sam said with a laugh, and Cameron smiled despite the seriousness of the conversation.

"No, you're not that bad. I was actually even a little glad you lost it and kicked me out when you did. It showed me you had a limit, and you weren't completely perfect."

Sam gave him a look like he clearly asked, "what are you smoking?" before he said, "Perfect? Not hardly. You lived with me for months. You had to have seen how *not* perfect I am, at least a few times. I know you've seen me first thing in the morning. I mean, come on." Cameron laughed with him, but they were getting off the subject, and he knew he hadn't really convinced Sam he was right yet.

He took a deep breath and tried again. "Sam, you're just going to have to trust me that I know the shit I'm capable of. It's already bad enough, now I have access to the guilt money. Just knowing it's there to fall back on makes me want to be lazy sometimes and not roll out of bed for work when I'm tired or when I've had a shitty day. Sometimes the only thing that stops me is how little there is left of it and the thought of you or Dr. Felicia being disappointed in me."

Sam chewed on his lip for a while, running his hand over Cameron's thigh, drawing distracting little patterns on his skin with his fingertips, while he stared down at the mattress pensively. After a while, he sighed and lifted his gaze. "I think I get it, even if I don't want to agree with it. So I'm not going to try to convince you otherwise, at least not yet. But believe me when I say that I think you're being too hard on yourself. I think you might surprise yourself one of these days."

Cameron wanted to cry, so he stretched out next to Sam and kissed him to avoid looking like a baby. "I want to be the person you see when you look at me," he whispered against Sam's lips.

"You already are," Sam whispered back.

It turned out Sam didn't really need twenty minutes to recuperate, after all. When Cameron pounced on him, the man was definitely up and ready to go. Cameron was on top again, figuratively as well as literally this time, and Sam came hard, locking his jaw tight to stifle his shout as Cameron fucked him through his orgasm before giving in to his own. Cameron was sure he saw stars before he collapsed on top of Sam, happier than he could ever remember being in his whole life. If only the rest of the world didn't exist, and he and Sam could stay like that forever. It was a nice thought, and he passed out with a smile on his face.

# CHAPTER SEVENTEEN

SAM WOKE with a stiff back and aching muscles in all kinds of unusual places. He rolled over on the hard futon mattress to find Cameron sleeping peacefully next to him, and he smiled, despite all the aches and pains. After the previous night, he was pretty sure keeping up with Cameron in the sack was either going to kill him or get him in the best shape of his life. At least he'd live or die a happy man.

He reached out and gently brushed Cameron's short, damp curls from his forehead. Sam hadn't really had time to tell him the night before, but he was glad Cameron had gotten rid of the black. Cameron was pretty enough he could probably pull off any hair color, but Sam kind of hoped he'd keep it natural for a while. The light brown looked really good on him.

As he lay there watching Cameron sleep, Sam suffered a "robbing the cradle" moment. Cameron looked even younger when he was sleeping, but Sam supposed he'd probably have to get used to feeling that way every once in a while, because he certainly wasn't going to change his mind, now he'd finally gotten Cameron back. Despite their age difference, they were good together. When it was just the two of them, everything was so easy. They laughed, they cooked, they played games, they had the same taste in movies, and they both loved all kinds of music. The only thing missing had been the sex. And now Sam knew how well they fit in bed, it was even more obvious to him they belonged together. If he could only convince Cameron to move back in with him, and convince everyone else he wasn't making a mistake, life would be golden.

As if the thought conjured them, Sam heard footsteps and whispering in the hall outside his door, signaling his guests were up and moving, and he should probably be doing the same. He didn't want to. He wanted to stay where he was and wake Cameron up the right way, but duty called. Ethan and Veronica were driving home that day, and it would be rude not to give them a proper send-off. Sam's *mamá* had trained him better than that.

He eased out of bed as gently as he could, pulled on his boxers and the robe he used only when he had guests in the house, and tiptoed to the bathroom. He brushed his teeth and hosed off a little, so he didn't smell quite so much like sex. A look in the mirror showed him a big goofy grin he couldn't quite get rid of, but he was fine with that. He was already prepared for Ethan to give him all kinds of shit anyway, so he might as well enjoy the afterglow while it lasted.

"Hey there. We were wondering if we'd see you at all before we left." The opening salvo came from Veronica instead of Ethan, catching Sam off guard, and he blushed. The happy couple was already outside, sitting on his deck with a couple of mugs of coffee. To hide his embarrassment, Sam simply waved and headed for the kitchen to get his own coffee, giving himself time for the blush to fade.

"You know I wouldn't let you go without saying good-bye," Sam finally replied as he joined them.

Veronica grinned knowingly at him, but Ethan didn't look amused, and Sam's goofy smile slipped. "Everything okay, Eth?"

Veronica tsked and patted her husband's arm. "Don't pay any attention to him. I know we've only seen each other a few times since the wedding, Sam, but last night was the happiest I've seen you since we met. *I* think that's all that matters, but Ethan thinks that's the mommy hormones talking." She stuck her tongue out at her husband, and Ethan finally cracked a smile.

His friend shook his head and turned to look at him. "Sorry, Sam. I worry about you sometimes. That's all. I remember what an ass you told me Keith turned out to be." He paused and pursed his lips. "Cameron seems like a nice kid. He's just so... *young.*"

Sam was pretty sure he was going to hear it a lot, so he needed to start getting used to dealing with it. At least Ethan was being nice about it. He shuddered to think what his *mamá* and Elena were going to say.

"I appreciate the concern, but Cameron is a good *man*, and he makes me happy. I've spent way too long without him, being unhappy, as it is. I'm a big boy. I can handle it."

Ethan quirked a smile and raised his mug to Sam and his wife in a toast, as Sam spotted Cameron shuffling into the living room over Ethan's shoulder. Cameron was fully dressed in the clothes he'd worn the day before, but he looked rumpled and sleepy, and hot enough Sam really wanted to forget his guests were there. Instead of embarrassing himself and his friends, however, Sam exercised restraint and let Cameron get his coffee on his own, waiting in his seat, like the grown-up he was, for Cameron to come out and join them.

"Good morning, Cameron. Did you sleep well?" Veronica asked, her face the picture of innocence.

Cameron blushed, and Sam was glad to know he wasn't the only one she could do that to. "Yeah, I slept great, thanks," he mumbled over the rim of his coffee mug, without looking in Sam's direction.

"Oh good. We did too," she replied a little too cheerily. "I woke up a couple of times, when I thought I heard something, but it must have been the wind." Ethan started coughing, Cameron nearly spit out his mouthful of coffee, and Sam cringed. He decided to change the subject before one or all of the men at the table died of embarrassment.

"I'm glad you guys slept well, Vee. Shouldn't you get started packing? I know it's a long drive home."

She rolled her eyes and pouted a little, but then she sighed and said, "Yeah, we probably should. The four-hour drive takes us about six because I have to stop every freaking half hour to pee and waddle around. I am definitely ready for our little bun to be finished baking in this oven." She grimaced and patted her belly before pushing herself to her feet. Ethan was right there to help her, hovering over her like she might collapse at any second, and Sam thought they both had never looked happier, even on their wedding day. Of course, it could be Sam was seeing everything through the hazy eyes of the love-struck and fully sated. A night of fantastic sex will do that to a guy. But he didn't care. His friends seemed happy. He was happy. Life was good.

His goofy smile was back and stayed with him, even as he said good-bye to them. It was there right up until Cameron turned to him with regret in his eyes and said, "I have to go. I have the afternoon shift at the coffee shop and a seven o'clock class after that. I've got to get home and get changed."

Sam pouted a little, but he pulled Cameron into his arms and kissed him slow and sweet anyway. "You programmed your number into my phone, right?" Cameron nodded. "And you put your address in there too?"

His lover smiled. "Yup."

Sam sighed and bumped their foreheads together. "Okay. E-mail me your schedule when you have it, and I'll see what I can do about getting time off when you're free, okay?" They hadn't really taken time to talk about this part, but Sam hoped he wasn't assuming too much by asking.

Cameron cupped his cheek and lifted those gorgeous hazel eyes to his as his smile widened. "Yeah, okay."

Neither one of them made any move to let go, so they stayed like that for a while until Sam wrapped his arms completely around Cameron and gave him one last squeeze. "Come on. I don't want to make you late the first time we're together. I'll never prove to you I can be a good influence that way. Let me walk you to your car."

They kissed a couple more times on the short walk out, before Sam reluctantly shoved his lover into his car and stepped back so he could drive away. As he watched the car disappear, Sam considered calling Cameron's cell to make sure he had the right number, but he didn't want to distract him while he was driving, and he didn't want to appear quite as clingy as he felt, not yet anyway. They had time now. He could be patient, sort of.


OVER THE next few weeks, they spent as much of their free time together as they realistically could. Sam still had his business and the classes he taught at the youth center, and Cameron was working two jobs, taking classes, and going to meetings with his therapist, as well as trying out an ACA group she'd recommended, so it wasn't easy. But they managed to squeeze in a few nights a week. They spent most of their time together at Sam's house, naked, or partially naked, or about to become naked. He'd been right about Cameron's libido. God, that boy was always horny. Sam was pretty sure he'd never known anyone that horny in his whole life. But he wasn't exactly complaining either. He kind of felt like a kid again, surprising even himself with his ability and willingness to keep up.

If they'd had a normal relationship from the start, Sam might have been a little concerned about the amount of time they were spending in bed—or on the floor, or the couch, or in the shower—together. But very little about their relationship was normal, and Sam figured they'd already gotten the "becoming friends" part out of the way early, so they had a little bit to catch up on in the lovers department.

They did more than make love, though. There were more cooking lessons and game nights. Although a few meals got burned beyond recognition when they were forgotten in favor of other things. And a few games took several nights to complete, because they kept getting paused for hours at a time. But they did finish the games eventually.

Their time in bed wasn't only about sex either. This time around, Sam wasn't going to repeat his past mistakes. He paid close attention, and he discovered early on Cameron seemed at his most willing to share when they were curled up together in the dark, and his lover was sated, relaxed, and happy. So if that was the best way to get Cameron talking, then Sam was going to take advantage of it as often as he could. The intimacies Cameron shared were well worth the days where Sam had to go to work on only a few hours' sleep.

Most of the time, they talked about simple things, everything from Cameron's classes and roommates, to crazy customers from both their jobs. But, every once in a while, his lover would open up about something important—sometimes good, sometimes painful—and those were the times Sam cherished most, because it meant Cameron was trusting him with a part of himself, and trust wasn't something Cameron gave lightly.

"Sam?" Cameron whispered in the dark one night, a month after they'd gotten together again.

It was mid-March, but a cold front had come in, dropping temperatures overnight into the low forties, and they were curled up under the quilt Sam's *abuela* had made for him, as well as the comforter he'd bought for his bedroom set.

"Yeah?" he said groggily. He'd started to drop off to sleep after another marathon, inspired by a bottle of Riesling and the can of whipped cream he'd bought for the peach cobbler recipe Cameron wanted to try.

"How come you haven't done anything with the money I gave you?"

*Uh oh.*

Sam struggled to wake himself up so he could think. "Uh, because you won't take it back?"

The envelope Cameron had brought him was still sitting on his dresser, and Sam now regretted leaving it out where his lover could see it.

Cameron sighed heavily and punched him lightly on the arm. "I won't take it back, because it's money I *owe* you. I worked hard for that, so it could come all from me—no guilt money—and I want you to have it."

Sam reached out in the dark and trailed his fingers soothingly over Cameron's arm, stalling. He didn't want the money. He didn't need it, and he knew Cameron did, but he didn't know how to say that without hurting his feelings, and he obviously wasn't awake enough to come up with anything brilliant now. "You never did tell me what happened with the guilt money," he said, changing the subject instead.

Cameron sighed again and scooted across the sheets, snuggling up to him, and Sam almost regretted bringing up the sensitive subject. Cameron always sought as much physical contact between them as possible whenever they talked about something he found painful. Sam was pretty proud of himself for actually picking up on that one without anyone having to point it out to him.

"My dad's lawyer did some checking with the bank, after some nasty e-mails back and forth with my mom, and he found out they'd been using the guilt money to pay their own bills. That's why they wouldn't let me have any of it and they got so touchy whenever I brought it up." Cameron scooted even closer. "Apparently '*the asshole*' took some hits on his investments when the economy went to shit, and they've been using the money to supplement his income, so they could continue to live in the style to which they had become accustomed."

Sam closed his eyes and wrapped his arms around him. "Shit. Seriously?"

Cameron's laugh was bitter. "Yeah. Tell me about it. They're going to put it all back, though. That's what they said anyway. But Mr. Garza threatened them with criminal charges, if they didn't get started right away. They gave him some sob story about how they were going to have the sell their house to do it, but I had him tell them I didn't care." Cameron paused, slid his arms around Sam's back and ran his hands in random patterns over Sam's skin for a while, and Sam knew to keep quiet until Cameron was ready to talk again. "They're not allowed to contact me directly anymore, you know. Everything's done through Mr. Garza's office, so I don't have to hear the worst of it. All I know is, there's an accountant involved, and he's figuring out how much was used for what it was intended, and he's going to send them a bill for the rest, and control has reverted to me, now that I'm twenty-one."

Sam kissed his forehead and stroked his back in the silence that followed. "Jesus, Cameron. I'm so sorry you had to go through that, after everything else they put you through."

Cameron was quiet for a little while longer before he squeezed Sam back and said, "Don't be. We've spent a lot of time on this in therapy, and I'm making peace with it, sort of. My mom gave up on being my mom a long time ago." He curled more tightly around Sam, twining their legs together and burying his face in Sam's neck. "She knew, you know," Cameron whispered against his skin. "... about my dad, I mean. Even after the divorce, I know she knew, and she never did anything until my dad got stupid and got caught messing with someone else's kid when I got too old for him. Even then, she wanted to keep it quiet, but the cops kept coming and eventually got the truth out of me. She had the fucking nerve to act shocked when they told her what I'd said."

Sam could tell Cameron was really getting upset now, so he kept quiet and just held him. That was the most he'd ever told Sam about what happened with his father, but Sam didn't mind. He really didn't want to know the details, unless Cameron needed tell him. It might be selfish of him, but Sam wasn't sure how he'd handle it if Cameron ever did. What little he knew already made him want to track all of them down and beat them until they begged Cameron for forgiveness, and then maybe beat them some more after that.

"I hate them. I hate all of them," Cameron whispered brokenly against his neck, and Sam closed his eyes on the tears that threatened.

"I hate them too, Cam. They deserve it," he whispered back, burying his face in Cameron's hair and holding him tighter.

Cameron shuddered a little in his arms, and Sam thought he heard a sniffle before his lover pulled away a little. Sam couldn't see it, but he felt Cameron tap his chest with a pointy finger a couple of times as he said, "You still didn't answer me about the money I gave you. Don't think I forgot about that," he laughed. It sounded forced, but Sam figured Cameron had just as much right to change the subject as he did, so he forced a chuckle as well.

"Okay, okay. I'll put it in the bank tomorrow. If that will make you happy."

"It will."

Sam pulled him down against his chest again. "You know I love you, right?"

Cameron kissed his chest. "I love you too, Sam, more than anyone," he said quietly.

The truth in those few words warmed him and broke his heart at the same time. Cameron truly didn't have anyone to love but him right now. He'd made some new friends at his work and school, and his roommates, Amber and Kaley, were pretty cool, but he didn't have a family yet. They were going to change that, though. Eventually, they would build a new family for Cameron together. Sam would make sure of it, no matter what.

They made love again that night, this time slow and sweet. Every touch and every kiss was tender, conveying more emotion than desire. They were lying on their sides, Cameron spooned against Sam's back, when Cameron finally pushed inside him. Sam twisted his shoulders so they could continue kissing and holding each other's faces as Cameron moved, fucking him in slow, steady strokes. It was perfect, and Sam never wanted it to end. But eventually, the need built, and Sam wrapped a hand around his own cock, pulling in time with Cameron's rhythm, as his lover sped toward a climax that shook them both and left them emotionally and physically exhausted, tangled together in the dark.

# CHAPTER EIGHTEEN

CAMERON PULLED up in front of Sam's house and cut the engine, but he didn't get out right away. He was nervous, almost as nervous as the day a couple of months before when he'd walked up to Sam's house with an envelope of money in one hand and his heart in the other.

Ryan and John were coming for dinner. It would be the first time he'd seen either of them since he'd moved out, and Cameron wasn't exactly looking forward to it. Sam promised he'd talked to Ryan, and the asshole had agreed to behave himself, but Cameron wasn't buying it. Things were going so fucking awesome with Sam right now, Cameron knew something shitty had to be coming. That was just how his life went.

He took a deep breath and forced himself to get out of the car. Ryan and John weren't there yet and wouldn't be for hours. Sam said he was leaving work early, but he wouldn't be home for at least another hour, so it wasn't like Cameron was walking into an ambush or something. He had plenty of time to chill out, get dinner started, and maybe drink a beer or three to relax.

That was actually a joke.

Tempting as the thought was, Cameron didn't want to be drunk when facing Ryan, and self-medicating never led to anything good—for him or anyone around him—a fact that had become abundantly clear in his therapy sessions, as well as his ACA meetings. But, just because preflighting was out didn't mean he couldn't lean on one of his other crutches, his favorite crutch actually, to relieve some stress. Cameron grinned to himself as he unlocked the front door and made his way to the kitchen. He could probably talk Sam into a quickie before their guests arrived. Sam was going to want a shower after work anyway, right?

As he fantasized about that, an idea occurred to him, and he grinned even broader. He quickly kicked off his boat shoes, pulled off his polo, and shimmied out of his skinny jeans, leaving nothing on but his purple-and-white Diesel boxer briefs. As he started getting things ready for dinner, he decided to put on the apron Sam had given him as a belated birthday present, because boiling water on naked skin was not a pleasant experience and burns were not particularly sexy. Besides, Cameron had to leave at least a couple of things for Sam to rip off of him.

Sam was appropriately appreciative of his outfit when he got home. In fact, it was a good thing Cameron had already finished cooking the rice, making the salad, and soaking the cedar plank for the grilled salmon, or dinner might have been considerably later than they'd planned. The apron was indeed ripped off, as were his briefs. But Sam surprised him by immediately dragging him into the shower, dropping to his knees, and taking Cameron's cock into his mouth before Cameron even had a chance to say, "Hi, honey, how was your day?"

Cameron leaned his head back against the tiles and groaned as Sam's lips and tongue moved over him. His man had an incredibly talented mouth, a fact he was glad he'd learned only after they'd finally gotten together or he would have gone crazy with waiting far sooner than he had.

Warm water rained over them as Sam took him deeper and deeper into his throat, bringing Cameron closer and closer to the edge, before easing back again teasing him. When Sam finally pulled off of him completely, Cameron's whine of complaint turned into a grunt of surprise as he was flipped around and shoved forward, barely able to throw his hands up to brace against the tile wall, before Sam was pulling his cheeks apart and a hot tongue was on his ass.

"Holy fuck!" Cameron grunted as his legs trembled and he scrabbled against the tiles, looking for purchase.

*Gawd, that tongue is talented.*

Cameron's cock was so hard and aching it throbbed against his belly with each thrust Sam made inside him, and his orgasm caught him completely by surprise. He hadn't even summoned the energy to reach down and grab his dick before he was shooting all over the tiles, and Sam was gloved and inside him an instant later. Cameron wasn't sure if he'd lost time, or if Sam was just that fast, and he didn't really care as his lover set a pounding rhythm.

It didn't last long. Sam had finally figured out, over the last few months, that Cameron wasn't fragile, despite his size. He wouldn't break, even if Sam really let go and fucked him hard. And this time it *was* hard... and fast, and so fucking hot, Cameron had a small, secondary orgasm that came out of nowhere. He felt it all the way to his toes when Sam shouted, "Aww, Christ!" and ground into him, lifting him up, off the tub, and holding him against the tile wall.

Cameron's legs were jelly when Sam finally set him back down, and he slumped onto the edge of the tub as Sam leaned against the back wall, laughing and panting.

"I was thinking waiting for you to come home in just an apron was a little too fifties housewife, but if that's what it gets me, fuck if I care what it looks like," Cameron said, when he could breathe again.

Sam laughed again and lifted Cameron into his arms, walking them both back under the spray. "It was hot, so fuck if I care what it looks like either," he said.

Sam grabbed the soap and began running it over both of their bodies. By the time Sam made it to shampooing Cameron's hair, Cam could feel himself getting hard again. He was considering his options when Sam said, in an oh so casual tone, "You know, if you moved back in with me, we could shower like this every day, conserve water and everything."

Cameron smiled and let his head drop back into Sam's strong hands as the man massaged his scalp. It was a topic that had come up many times over the months since they'd finally hooked up, although

Sam usually wasn't so blatant about it. But Sam was beginning to wear him down, especially since Cameron really didn't want to say no, and even Felicia didn't think it was such a bad idea anymore. Sam sat in on a few of their sessions, and Dr. Felicia warmed up to him right away. Now if his therapist wasn't immune to Sam's charms, what chance did Cameron have of holding out? But Cameron couldn't be sure if he and Sam were both convincing her living with him was a good idea because Cameron wanted it so bad, or because his fears were truly unfounded. And until he was, he couldn't say yes.

Cameron straightened and moved his head under the spray, rinsing out the soap before leaning forward and kissing Sam on the lips. "I know. And you know I've been thinking about it. Let's just get through tonight, okay?"

Sam gave him a sheepish smile and nodded. "Yeah, okay."

Cameron turned to step out of the tub but yelped a second later when Sam's hand gave him a resounding smack on the ass. He turned around rubbing the offended cheek and glared at Sam, who stood grinning back at him.

"I'll be out in a minute," Sam said, completely unrepentant.

Cameron harrumphed and scooted out of range, frowning at his lover's back, but secretly a little pleased. He'd actually kind of liked it. They might have to explore that sometime when they didn't have guests coming.

Thoughts of being spread out on Sam's bed with his ass in the air as the man spanked him started to make him hard again as he made his way through the living room, ducking low so no one could spot him through the front window without his clothes on. His clothes were where he'd left them, on the floor by the kitchen, and he pulled them back on before finishing the prep work for dinner, hoping his dick would relax before their guests arrived. He cranked up the music on Sam's new stereo system to try to keep his mind off the naked man at the back of the house and got back to work.

Sam joined him a little while later, and they behaved themselves as they finished the cooking and cleanup. Cameron was pulling the brie en croute he'd made with prepackaged puff pastry and dried cranberries out of the oven when the doorbell rang.

Did he have perfect timing or what?

It helped that John was apparently very anal about punctuality, so they knew exactly when their guests would be arriving. Cameron imagined most Angelenos would consider the man practically unhinged to expect people to actually show up on time to anything, but he had to admit it came in handy when he wanted to impress. Cameron set the brie on a plate and pulled off his oven mitts as Sam led their guests to the kitchen and poured them each a cocktail from the pitcher of pomegranate mojitos he'd made.

"Thanks," John said as he took the glass that was offered to him. "And how are you, Cameron?"

"I'm good." Cameron glanced at Sam. "Really good."

John's smile was wide as he looked between the two of them. "I'm glad to hear it. It's been a long time. You'll have to tell us about your classes and all that. Sam says you're doing really well."

"I'm doing okay," he replied, casting a nervous glance at Ryan before taking a sip from his drink.

Ryan wasn't exactly looking warm and welcoming, like John was obviously trying to be, but he wasn't quite hostile either, so Cameron figured that was a step up.

There was an awkward silence then, as Sam watched Ryan, and his welcoming smile started to fade. But before the evening could fall flat, five minutes after it started, John walked over and wrapped an arm around his partner, giving his lover a loud smack on the lips and beaming over at Cameron and Sam. "Why don't we grab this," he said, handing his drink to Ryan and reaching for the plate with the brie, "and we can all head over to the couch and catch up."

"Good plan," Sam agreed a little overly enthusiastically, grabbing the plate of apples they'd already cut up and winking at Cameron as he followed their guests to the couch. It was only April, and the nights were a little cool to be sitting out on the deck, so they were going to be trapped inside with Ryan for the whole night. Cameron had been the one to make that decision, but now he was regretting it.

Sam always laughed whenever Cameron complained about being cold. Sam was like a furnace most of the time and he'd already warned Cameron never to say anything about being cold in front of his mom, or she'd take fattening him up as her own private mission in life, and she wouldn't leave until she'd accomplished it. Maria Esperanza Hernandez Powell sounded like a sweet woman from everything Sam had told him, but Cameron wasn't sure he was ready for that kind of mothering yet. Sam's *mamá* was coming in a few weeks for a visit as it was and Cameron didn't need any more fuel for his anxiety. Psyching himself up for tonight had been hard enough.

Cameron had never realized being in love would turn out to be so hard. The loving Sam part was easy. They fit together so great, and he was happier than he'd been in his entire life every moment they spent alone together. It was all the other stuff that came with it that Cameron worried about: the close-knit family, the meddling friends. There were so many ways he could fuck up. Cameron was glad all that complicated bullshit had never occurred to him, or he might have been too afraid to even try with Sam. Now, he had no choice but to learn to deal with it.

Cam took another sip of his drink and a long, deep breath, before pulling the toasted bread rounds out of the oven and dumping them into the little basket he'd bought especially for this dinner party. Sam smiled and winked at him as Cameron set it down on the coffee table, and then Cameron sat on the floor at Sam's feet, leaning back against his legs.

Apparently neither one of their guests had been back to Sam's house since he'd bought the new furniture, because they both commented on how much they liked it as they dug in to the appetizer. Cameron was pretty sure *he* was the reason Sam's friends hadn't been over, and he felt a little guilty about that. Of course, he also still felt guilty every time he looked at the couch and all of the rest of the new stuff Sam had to buy. So, really, what was one more niggle of guilt in the whole scheme of things, right? Another reason to add to the list of why he shouldn't move back in. He needed to be sure he'd never hurt Sam like that again, and he wasn't there yet.

"So, Cameron, what classes are you taking now?" Ryan asked. Cameron didn't miss that John's hand had dropped to his lover's knee and given it a quick squeeze before the man spoke.

Cameron swallowed what was in his mouth and cleared his throat. "Just the basics right now: math and English. I have to build up some credits and get some good grades in before I can think about applying to anything beyond the community college."

He felt a little self-conscious talking about it with Sam's friends, since they were already professionals and college graduates. But Sam dropped a hand to his shoulder and smiled down at him, the pride obvious in his face, and Cameron felt most of the tension leave his body.

"He's doing great. A lot better than I ever did in school," Sam said, "I help him study sometimes, and I'm learning a lot of stuff I've either forgotten or never really learned in the first place. Makes me almost want to go and take a couple of classes myself, if it didn't mean we'd never have any time to spend together."

The conversation flowed a little easier after that. They talked about some of Ryan and John's favorite classes and professors when they were in school. They talked about work and some of Sam's other friends, and Cameron tried to build a memory bank for when he met them. He'd probably already been introduced to them at Sam's birthday party, but that was a night he'd rather forget, so Cameron was going to start over and pretend any or all of the people he was hearing about were complete strangers and hadn't ignored him or looked down on him.

By the end of the night, the pitcher of mojitos was empty and everybody seemed to be having a pretty good time, talking and laughing. Cameron had relaxed and was actually beginning to think they could all be friends, moving forward, until Ryan followed him into the kitchen when Cameron started cleaning up. Cameron tensed up immediately when he realized they were alone and John and Sam were still laughing and carrying on in the dining room. He eyed Ryan warily as he began to rinse plates and fill the dishwasher.

When Cameron continued to stare at him without saying anything, Ryan sighed loudly and rolled his eyes. "Look, Sam was pissed at me for more than a month, a new record for him. And John had me sleeping in the guest room for weeks, so you don't have to look at me like I'm going to bite your head off. I learned my lesson, and I fully intend to keep any negative opinions I might have to myself from now on, okay? I'm an asshole. I know I'm an asshole. But as long as Sam's happy, that's really all that matters."

"It's all that matters to me," Cameron said, straightening to his full height, which wasn't that impressive, but Ryan was the same height, so they were eye to eye.

"Good. It's all that matters to me too. We have something in common. You promise to never touch my boyfriend again, and maybe you and I can, if not be *friends*, at least get along well enough for Sam's sake."

"I can do that."

"Then I guess we have a deal," he said, and then he actually smiled as he held out the platter he was carrying and turned to go finish clearing the table.

Sam must have noted their absence because he came out of the dining room as Ryan was going in and looked at Cameron with concern in his eyes. "Everything okay?"

"Yeah, I think so. Everything okay with you?"

Sam smiled and his eyes were very warm as he said, "Yeah. Everything is pretty damned good with me."

Cameron wasn't sure if it was the alcohol or the company, but Sam spooned him close and held on tight all night after their guests went home. Cameron didn't mind in the slightest. There was no way he'd get cold with a Sam blanket wrapped around him.

He woke up only once, right after dawn, when Sam climbed on top of him, bracing his arms on either side of Cameron's head and smiling down at him.

Cameron smiled back, but when Sam stayed like that, he raised an eyebrow. "What?"

Sam shook his head. "I'm just happy. You make me so happy."

Great, Sam was getting mushy first thing in the morning, when Cameron wasn't awake enough to have his defenses up. The man always seemed to know the perfect time to strike. Cameron cleared his throat, trying to dislodge the lump that was forming, and rolled his eyes. "You couldn't wait until a decent hour to tell me that?"

Sam grinned back at him and began petting Cameron's hair, completely unrepentant. "Nope." He paused then, and his face sobered a little. "I know last night wasn't easy for you. I wanted to thank you for everything you did. Ryan was a real dick to you from the start, and you still worked hard to make them feel welcome. I know you did that for me. And it makes me love you even more."

Score one for team Cameron.

Before he could burst into tears and get Sam started crying too, Cameron wrapped his arms around Sam's neck and pulled him down for some kissing. They made out like that, morning breath and all, until neither one of them gave a damn what time it was, and all they could taste was the salt of each other's skin. Cameron wrapped his legs around Sam's hips and they made love until they passed out.

When Cameron woke up again, Sam was gone—cooking bacon in the kitchen by the smell of it. Cameron stretched out in their bed and listened to the faint sounds of the stereo and Sam puttering around in the kitchen, and it started him thinking. Maybe he *was* being a chickenshit about the whole moving back in thing. He'd survived the night with Ryan, and he thought he'd done pretty well there. He only had a couple more months on his lease with Amber and Kaley, and after that, there was nothing really keeping him there except for the fact that the commute from Sam's to his jobs and the school sucked. But he was making that trip several times a week anyway, so what was the difference?

He'd been thinking about this every day for months. Maybe it was time to trust himself a little more. Maybe it was time to have a little faith. He was still fucked-up, and probably always would be, just like dear old Art had said. But he knew a lot of fucked-up people, almost everyone he'd ever met actually. It was LA, after all. That didn't necessarily mean they couldn't have good lives. Cameron had all kinds of good people in his life now. He wasn't doing any of the things that got him in trouble in the past, and he was happier than he'd ever been. Sam didn't want him to be perfect. Sam just wanted *him*. He'd said so often enough, maybe it was time to believe him.

Cameron smiled up at the ceiling as he made his decision. He wouldn't tell Sam yet. He'd wait until after Sam's mom's visit, just in case something went horribly wrong and she hated him or something. But he was going to do it. As soon as his lease was up, he'd move back in with Sam. Maybe he'd write that on the birthday card and give it to Sam along with the new guitar he planned to buy for him. That would work, right? And then they'd figure things out from there... one step at a time.

ROWAN MCALLISTER is a woman who doesn't so much create as recreate, taking things ignored and overlooked and hopefully making them into something magical and mortal. She believes it's all in how you look at it. In addition to a continuing love affair with words, she creates art out of fabric, metal, wood, stone, and any other interesting scraps of life she can get her hands on. Everything is simply one perspective change and a little bit of effort away from becoming a work of art that is both beautiful and functional. She lives in the woods, on the very edge of suburbia—where civilization drops off and nature takes over—sharing her home with her patient, loving, and grounded husband, her super sweet hairball of cat, and a mythological beast masquerading as a dog. Her chosen family is made up of a madcap collection of people from many different walks of life, all of whom act as her muses in so many ways, and she would be lost without them.

E-mail: rowanmcallister10@gmail.com
Facebook: https://www.facebook.com/rowanmcallister10
Twitter: https://twitter.com/RowanMcallister

Also from ROWAN MCALLISTER

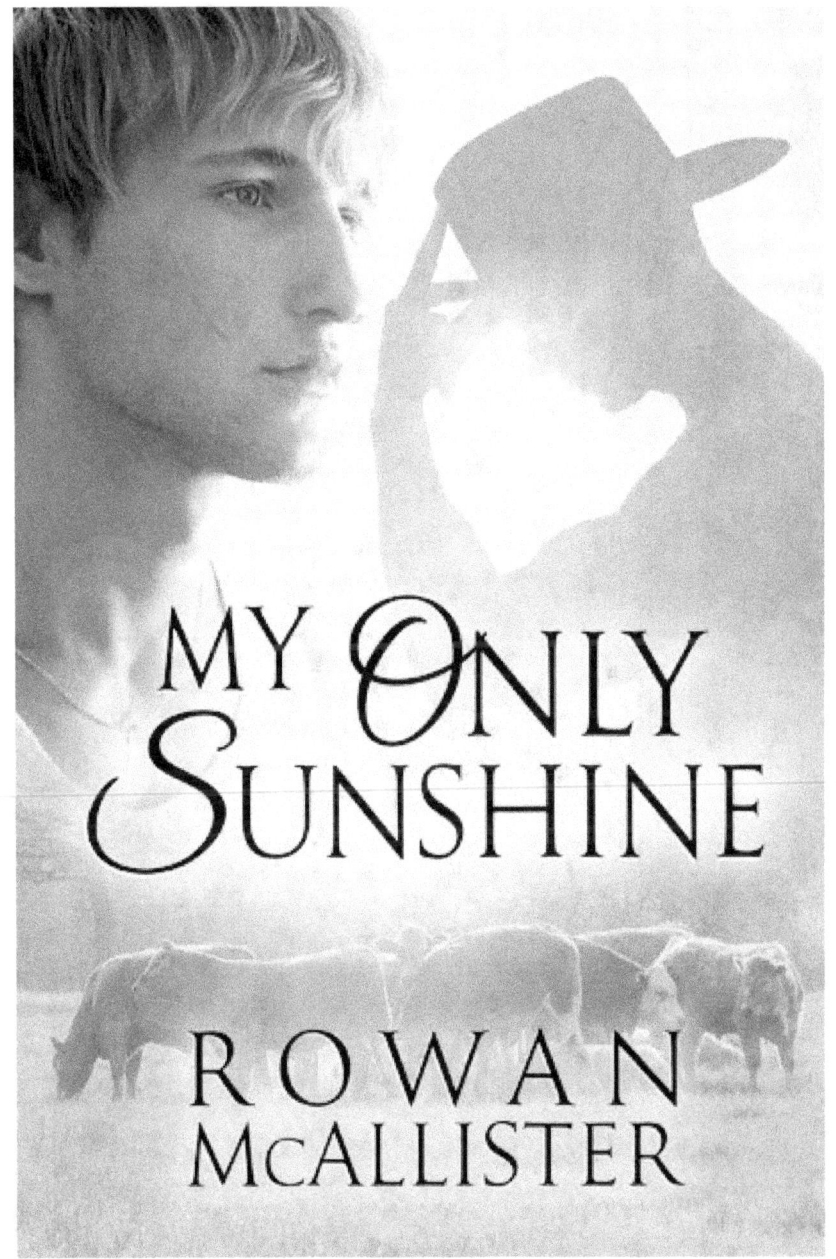

MY ONLY
SUNSHINE

ROWAN
MCALLISTER

http://www.dreamspinnerpress.com

Also from ROWAN MCALLISTER

http://www.dreamspinnerpress.com

www.ingramcontent.com/pod-product-compliance
Lightning Source LLC
Chambersburg PA
CBHW060059260626
47160CB00005B/1724